SEASON OF MISTS

G. Lowell Tollefson

LLT Press
P.O. Box 378
Eagle Nest, New Mexico 87718

ISBN-13: 978-0692470176 (LLT Press)
ISBN-10: 0692470174

Cover design: Loretta Miles Tollefson
Cover image: pixabay.com/en/shepherd-people-buffalo-forest-625903/

PRONUNCIATION KEY

Vietnamese is a tonal language. Thus the manner in which the voice rises, falls or repeats a vowel sound in a word determines its meaning. As a matter of convenience in reading, the names listed below are given *approximate* English pronunciations without regard for tonal variation or slight differences between the Northern and Southern dialects. In Vietnamese the family name is placed first in written or spoken order, the given name last. The letter combination *ng* placed at the beginning of a Vietnamese word is pronounced like the same combination at the end of the English word *swimming*. I have simply rendered it as an *n* sound here.

Characters

Nguyen Duc Thuy	Nūyĕn Dŭk Twē	(main protagonist)
Nguyen Chi Lan	Nūyĕn Chē Lăn	(Duc Thuy's sister)
Quong Anh Thuy	Kwŭng Ăn Twē	(Communist Party cadre)
Vo Ngoc Loan	Vō Năk Lōăn	(Viet Cong company commander)
Quoc Duong Li	Kwŭk Dūŭng Lē	(contact man at Dai Loc)
Vuong Gia Ki	Vūŭng Gēă Kē [hard G]	(young friend of Duc Thuy)

Place Names

Quang Nam	Kwăng Năm	(province)
Dai Loc	Dăē Lăk	(village, district)
Song Xuong Ca	Sōng Sūŭng Kă	(Fish Bone river)
Song Thu Bon	Sōng Tū Bōn	(Thu Bon river)

SEASON OF MISTS

MISTS

G. Lowell Tollefson

I

The sun was always hot well past midday in the village of Xuong Ca. It was the warm season and the grass was green on the dikes between the fields. The time for replanting had come, and the young rice was ready for the stronger men and women, laboring long in the sun, to put into the fields. This was done in the earlier part of the day. Now some of the old men fished for shrimp, carp and minnows in the few paddies which had already been flooded and enriched with new plants. The flooding for the newly planted fields had been accomplished by people pouring water in straw buckets from one rice paddy to another. Others pulled up weeds among corn plants in dry fields. A few older women worked in garden plots. But most of the people on this late afternoon were out cutting palm leaves on the bank of the nearby river, in the forest breaks, and along the borders of the fields. Throughout the area, a rich tangle of jungle tumbled into every open space, as if to reclaim it. Cocks crowed, a dog barked, smoke rose hazily from a thatch hut hidden by trees, and the brown Song Xuong Ca, or Fish Bone river, unseen from the fields, rolled its muddy waters not more than a stone's throw away in the jungle beyond the double row of thatch houses that was the village.

Nguyen Duc Thuy was sixteen. He was helping the others bring in the bundles of palm leaf, which would be used to repair the thatch roofs of the houses. His fifteen year old sister, Nguyen Chi Lan, was helping also. In the distant hills American artillery could be heard, and at one point Thuy stopped, setting down his load, cupping his hand over his eyes, and watched two silver specks rise and fall in the distance, pummeling a village with bombs. Black puffs of smoke hung over the trees.

"They will not come to attack us?" Lan asked.

"No, I do not think so."

"But they are closer today."

"They do not care about us."

Thuy picked up his bundle and walked to the village. Lan followed him. They stacked their bundles beside the family hut. Inside, their mother was turning the fire coals and their father sat in the doorway. He often sat thus, when the attacks of malaria came upon him. Sometimes he lay indoors in a sweat, trying to keep cool.

"How are you doing, father?" Thuy asked. His father nodded but did not answer. Thuy went into the hut.

"They will not kill the only son and daughter I have left," his mother said without rising.

"No, they will not come here. They do not care about us."

"They killed your uncle and your father's mother too."

"That was the French."

"It is all the same."

There were two rooms in the hut. Thuy went into the second room. Several wooden beds stood along the wall partitions with bamboo mats rolled up at the foot of them. It was cool and dark in the room. Thuy knelt down beside one of the beds. Beneath it was a pit, several feet deep and the length of the bed. This was for bomb and artillery attacks. One simply rolled off the bed into it. Each bed had one. Every bed in the village had one. But it had been a number of years since the war had touched Xuong Ca. Though the war raged within seeing and hearing distance of them day and night, the village was like an island in the green jungle, safely off the main transportation routes. Only

Viet Cong and an occasional North Vietnamese unit came through, but the Americans were not aware of their presence here, a particularly low density population area, a region of poor farming and dense jungle.

Thuy reached into the pit under his bed. Still wrapped in the original plastic bag and heavily coated with Cosmoline jelly was a new "SKS," a Chinese carbine rifle. Thuy had had the weapon for several weeks, as did several other boys and young men in the village. This was something new to them, for only recently a Communist party political cadre had taken up residence there. He held regular meetings for those who wished to attend, and it was he who was responsible for procuring the weapons, which had been smuggled in from Laos. When he, Quong Anh Thuy, for his name was also Thuy, had first taken up residence there, everyone had been curious. But over the months only a few remained interested enough to continue attending his meetings. Marxist doctrine, even in greatly simplified form, did not appeal to men and women who had labored many years in the fields, could not read and write, and had never been more than a few miles from home. The absentee landlord who took so large a portion of their labor in his fields was simply a fact of life, like the slow, hot, muggy, daily movement of the sun, which one complained about often but never expected to change.

But with the young it was different. They were eager, full of hope and a sense of injured justice, though not one of these boys and young men had yet seen combat against Americans. They were quickly recruited, almost to a man, between the ages of sixteen and thirty—those at least who did not have families. Some had already left the village to join the local Viet Cong unit.

Thuy's mother knew of the rifle, but his father and sister did not. He examined the plastic wrapper without removing its contents, replaced it in the pit and returned to the outer room. His mother turned and looked up at him, still squatting near the fire. Her eyes were dark brown, deep and full of pain, pain for a grief which had not occurred. Thuy smiled, touched her cheek and left the hut.

II

They had gathered in a small clearing in the jungle not far from the village: four boys and seven young men. Thuy, the local party representative, was explaining some of the difficulties of Marxist thought. He sat in the dark with his legs crossed, the eleven volunteers ringed in a half circle in front of him.

"The common working man in this country," he said, "is a farmer, for those living in the cities are mostly corrupt."

None of the young volunteers had ever seen a city. They imagined a place of tremendous licentiousness and noise, of wild physical abandonment, crowds of men and women jostling together for the pleasures of this world. They listened in silence.

"It is up to the farmer to free his people," Thuy continued. "Only he has the discipline of routine, hardship and labor that creates self-control. Only he knows of the suffering that the Americans, and the French before them, have brought upon the common people of this land. We will throw them out, every usurper of Vietnamese freedom. The Chinese are our friends now and want to help us. But we must never forget that we are Vietnamese. They all bring foreign power to oppress us, and they set Vietnamese over Vietnamese, turning brother against brother to make it easier for them to exploit us. They create rich and lazy people who live in the cities and do no work but eat the labor of our hands. They give them guns to attack us if we resist, and they take away young men from our homes to fight against those who would free us. But each day the people, the true Vietnamese of the countryside who work with their hands and share in the fruits of common labor, grow stronger. The more we are oppressed, the more foreigners come here to kill us, the stronger we become. Their guns and bombs kill the body, not the soul of a people."

Anh Thuy was a man in his late thirties. When he spoke, he pronounced his words slowly and deliberately, as though choosing them from a reservoir of deep experience. It is true that he himself had never read Marx or Engels or Lenin or Mao Tse-Tung, but it was not the doctrine of textbook philosophy he had come to deliver. The people had their philosophy, Taoist and Buddhist. What they wanted was a clear understanding of their present misfortune. Then they would act. It had always been so. It had been so when the Chinese yoke had been cast off time and again. It was thus with the defeat of the French. And now the Americans had come to learn of the strength of village truth—the Americans who thought governments in cities, far removed from the rhythms of rice paddy and corn field, spoke and acted for the people.

Young Thuy was excited that night. He had made a final decision. The sound of artillery rumbling in the distance quickened him. It made his heart pound in the dark. He wondered if his voice would quaver when he spoke. It did not.

"Brother Thuy," he began. The party cadre had encouraged his new adherents to use this familiar form of address. "Brother Thuy, I am prepared to leave my home in the service of freedom."

"Does your father know of this?"

"He does not. But I will inform him."

"And if he objects."

"Then I will insist—with the great respect that is due to my father."

"This is no light matter, younger Thuy, for there will be many hardships and privations. It is likely you may be killed, as is the case even now with some of your noble village brothers who have gone before you. The Americans have many and powerful weapons. We have but few and they are simple, such as can be carried by men on foot or transported upon the back of an occasional elephant."

"We do not need the big guns and airships of the Americans. We will defeat them with our hearts. If I fall, another shall soon follow, and another and another."

The party cadre looked long and intently at the boy. Though his expression was as smooth as flax, he smiled inwardly, for these were his own words.

"Good," he said with a short nod. "In the morning after tomorrow a patrol will arrive in the village for resupply. You will go with them. Do not forget your weapon."

Shortly thereafter they all rose and returned to the village. As they were walking along, young Thuy lagged behind the others until the cadre, who was yet further in the rear, caught up with him. The boy did not know what it was he wished to say and before he could think to speak was surprised to learn that the party cadre would be going with him. It seemed the Viet Cong unit was now sufficiently resupplied to return to action, and its strength had been rebuilt to about thirty men. Those who were left behind in the village with weapons would be given a small amount of ammunition when the patrol came. If any Americans came through, they could act as guerrillas, harassing them. A disabled comrade from a previous campaign, who was already lodged in the village, would demonstrate to them the proper assembly and use of their new weapons.

Thuy did not say anything to his father. The fever and intermittent chills had worsened and he was too sick. Nor did Thuy speak of the matter to his mother or his sister. His sister knew nothing. On the evening before the arrival of the patrol, as Chi Lan knelt on the dirt floor inside the main room of the hut, carefully searching for lice in her mother's hair, which she deftly extracted with her fingers and cracked with her teeth, Thuy entered.

"I wish to be alone for a moment," he said, nodding toward their mother. Lan got up and quietly left. Outside several dogs were barking at the arrival of some men from another village. The air was beginning to cool, and the sun glared red through the tops of the trees west of the village.

Thuy squatted and put his arm around his mother, who sat with her legs gathered to one side. Her black cotton peasant's pajama bottoms were dusty, and her white cotton blouse was smudged in several places from the day's work. There was a small hole on her left shoulder, caused by the material having been beaten threadbare by heavy rocks during washing. She did not look up at her son. He did not have to tell her he was leaving. The only consolation there was to fill her heart was the hatred she bore for every foreigner.

III

Thuy did not begin his career as a main line combatant. His youth and inexperience needed months of conditioning. Because of the number of new recruits in its ranks, his company located itself at first in a hilly region of jungle not more than ten miles from an American outpost. Here their initial training was supplied largely by the enemy.

Moving from base camp to base camp, composed mostly of complex networks of underground tunnels where the men slept, ate and stashed their weapons and supplies, they were bombarded daily. The Americans knew there was much activity in the area, and the artillery barrages and sporadic bombings were part of a random strategy referred to as "harassment and interdiction fire." When centered in populated areas infested with supposed Viet Cong activity, it took many civilian lives. But the loss in casualties among soldiers of the people's army was always slight. It seemed to serve little other purpose than to toughen them, to inure them to fear, hardship and the rigors of an incessantly mobile, underground life.

The men learned to live from day to day, carrying their ration of rice wrapped in a bundle about their stomachs. Some of the underground base camps were large enough to have a small staff of two or three young female nurses. These "nurses" not only treated illness and dressed occasional wounds but cooked up the rice, adding foodstuffs gathered in the surrounding jungles or from an occasional foray into a distant village. They too were highly mobile and moved from base camp to base camp. During this period, Thuy and his comrades were instructed in party doctrine by the cadre and were familiarized by the experienced soldiers in the use and assembly of various weapons—from automatic rifles and mortars to one hundred twenty millimeter rockets.

Finally, after a couple months of this, they entered the second phase of their training. They became porters, carrying rice and supplies from distant villages to the jungle, where it was stashed in the base camps. They also picked up weapons and ammunition in the base camps and transported them to underground caches in or near villages in the combat area, under the very nose of the Americans. This they did almost entirely at night, sometimes pressing the local villagers temporarily into service as carriers. On such occasions Thuy and his comrades acted as guards for the sometimes unwilling coolies. For though not strictly offensive or combatant in nature, this duty was extremely dangerous. The Americans in the region were Marines, who would honeycomb the area with night ambush patrols. If you stumbled into one of these, you were walking into a veritable wall of flaming red. These Americans spared no ammunition in a fight and seemed to possess unlimited quantities of it. Later Thuy would learn, among other things, how to draw out such fire to frustrate the Americans and tax their supplies, increasing their sense of futility in fighting an ever-present and seemingly invisible opponent.

The soldiers of the hard core guerrilla units—that is, those who were not simple farmers acting part time as fighters—moved about continually. They would mass in an area, combining smaller units to carry out operations against American outposts, then dissolve into separate units again as the Americans came out in pursuit. During periods of dispersal, tactical coordination was maintained by the political cadres attached to the companies, who sometimes met with other cadres at prearranged locations to discuss strategy and learn of general directives from the government in Hanoi. More often they communicated by messenger or left information with sympathizers when passing through a village, knowing other units would soon come through the same hamlet. This general fluidity of the Communists confused the Americans. It was all their intelligence specialists could do, with the combination of facts and misinformation gathered from captured weapons, documents and "usually reliable sources," to keep a running estimate of troop movements. This estimate generally amounted to little more than a vague idea of the types and numbers of regular North Vietnamese army units moving into the south. All in all, the guerrillas were like a fog to them, gathered here and there in the pockets of valleys, arising unexpectedly in the congealing night and dissipating into seeming nothingness with the first exposure to light.

During his period of service as a porter, young Thuy grew in strength of nerve, experience and wisdom. Though one of the youngest members of his company, his dedication and coolness did not escape notice. His interest in the homely philosophy of the party cadre drew them close. The elder Thuy was a Northerner and had lost his parents in a bombing raid. He had now been in the South for several years, and his harsher pronunciation of vowels and consonants, characteristic of the Hanoi dialect, had softened somewhat, blending with the more languid expression of Saigon. This was ideal, for he was located in the northernmost region of South Vietnam, in Quang Nam province, an area of mixed pronunciation precisely like his and with a few peculiarities of its own. He blended in like a native, and this was good for morale, since most of the men in his company were Southerners.

Though something of an expert on military tactics, Anh Thuy was not the company commander. In the development of specific details for carrying out an operation, he had to defer to Vo Ngoc Loan, a tough, somewhat embittered man in his forties. Loan was not much of a talker except when giving orders or settling tactical matters, but he seemed to have no knowledge of fear and was as patient as a Buddhist monk practicing the last of the Four Noble Truths. He was also careful about losses, though this seemed to result more from a need to win battles and deny those losses to the enemy than from a desire to save lives.

Anh Thuy, on the other hand, was a strategist, more in possession of the big picture, or overall plan, timely bits and pieces of which he received from the North in the manner already described. It was in such a capacity that he had need of a reliable young ward, and Duc Thuy soon became his man. They were now settled in an underground cavern discussing just such a mission. Three of them, Anh Thuy, Duc Thuy and the company commander were gathered together. A candle lit the spare earthen room in which the commander squatted and the other two sat cross legged on the dirt floor with a map unfolded between them. It was early nightfall and the smell of cooked rice drifted in from a passageway. The candle flickered as the ground trembled from an artillery barrage whistling in overhead, and bits of dust and clods of dirt were continually falling onto the three men from the roof and walls of the cavern.

"You are aware, young Thuy, that we shall soon begin regular military operations?" Ngoc Loan asked.

"No, I did not know."

"Anh Thuy informs me that there is a series of coordinated assaults planned for this region. We are to strike here." He pointed to a spot on the map. It was the Dai Loc district headquarters for the South Vietnamese government, but Duc Thuy could not read. Still he understood terrain designations and figures and could make out coordinates, Anh Thuy having taught him this skill in the preceding months.

"It is sixteen kilometers from here. Before we begin operations, we must have a precise knowledge of enemy strength and fortifications. You will go alone and make contact with a man named Quoc Duong Li. He is living in the village which is headquarters for the district. From him you will learn about troop strength. Then you will enter the American compound and make an assessment of fortifications. I want to know such things as the condition of the barbed wire on their perimeter, the character of troop approaches for our possible use, and the location of their sleeping quarters, mess hall and ammunition dump. Do they have any trucks, and what kind of guns do they have?" Loan sat back and looked calmly at Duc Thuy. "If you have not returned in two weeks, I will send another in your place," he added.

Duc Thuy made an effort to control the look of surprise on his face. He had never been asked to go on any kind of independent mission, and this, was this even possible?

Ngoc Loan picked up the map, folded it and put it into his khaki shirt pocket. He said nothing further and seemed to consider the discussion to be at an end. Duc Thuy looked at Anh Thuy.

"It is dangerous but not so difficult as it seems," the cadre said. "You will go first to Duong Li. He is well known and you will have no trouble finding him. He has also proven to be trustworthy. You will stay with him. There is a company of sappers which have been operating for some time in the area. They are experienced and very good. Only recently they were able to blow up a bridge and overrun the perimeter of another American unit without taking a single loss. They had reliable information such as you will provide. They have given much valuable knowledge to Duong Li concerning troop strengths at the American battalion headquarters. This they have obtained by estimate from numerous night probing actions. It is believed there are not more than two hundred men inside the hilltop compound these Americans occupy. They keep a light guard on their perimeter, and when attacked several minutes are required before these men are reinforced. This we already know, for Duong Li is in communication with the sapper company and has thus informed us. He will give you any further information he has received. Then it is up to you to augment this by getting inside the compound. A road passes through the middle of the compound, and you may find a means to convince the Americans that you need to pass through. We are sending you because you are young and can pass for a village youth. Allow yourself to be plainly seen in the village for several days, then make the attempt. We are very much in need of whatever you can find out."

At this point the artillery pounding had stopped. Ngoc Loan had already gotten up and scuttled down the passageway toward the smell of cooking rice. The passageway was narrow and not deep enough for a man to stand up in. One had to stoop or crawl to get from cavern to cavern.

"Let us fill our bellies," Anh Thuy said, smiling. He led the way in the direction the company commander had gone.

~ 15 ~

IV

Duc Thuy loved the jungle. This—for he was already in the lowlands—was not the high canopy forest of the hills, dominated by huge, broad based teak and ebony trees that, by shutting out light, made the underlying growth sparser and the forest seem like a large enclosed vault, cool and dim with thick, ropy lianas and vines hanging down. It was scrub jungle near the sea. Its growth was so thick and tangled one man could not see another in it at a distance of three yards. The Americans avoided it as much as possible and traveled through the open fields and rice paddies. This made it easy for guerrillas to set booby traps, knowing pretty much what routes American patrols would take and the fact that the more inexperienced ones would inevitably travel along the dikes separating rice paddies. A few plastic explosives and a wire strung carefully in the grass is all it would take. Boom! and there was a one-legged American imperialist yelling for help. Thuy smiled at the thought. This was not something he had seen but had only heard about. He had not even seen any Americans yet, since he had done most of his traveling through this country at night.

On his journey, besides rice, he was carrying the makings for a few such booby traps: four or five in all. He put them here and there when occasion admitted. It was while planting the last one in the middle of an open field that he got caught. That is, he was seen. He was running a wire in the water about three feet to one side of a dike. This was for some wiser patrol that might have learned to stay off the dikes themselves. While squatted down, fastening the wire horizontally to two bunches of rice stalks at a point just below the surface of the water, he heard a droning noise. A light bodied, propeller driven spotter plane seemed to have appeared out of nowhere. At first it was like a bird far up in the wide expanse of blinding blue sky. Then it dropped down over a nearby tree line and headed straight for him. Young Thuy did not know what to make of this, which way to run. He was in the middle of a conflux of several fields. The nearest copse of trees was a good hundred yards off. Was this light plane armed with machine guns?

Thuy threw himself behind the dike as the plane buzzed over him. The pilot had to know he was a guerrilla fighter. He was armed with a rifle, and he certainly was not out there all by himself planting rice. The plane did not strafe him. Thuy knew this probably meant the pilot had merely come down for a closer look, had already fixed his position and was even now calling in an artillery barrage. Thuy's heart raced wildly. Thinking was difficult. His temples throbbed, but he did not lose control. He had to make it to the nearest copse of trees. Any spot on earth was preferable to the one he was in. He thought he could hear the screaming shells, but he was standing now and nothing struck. Then he noticed a strange thing. The plane had actually come down in an adjacent field. It had landed, and the pilot was climbing out of it, a rifle slung over his shoulder. The man was apparently planning to capture him single-handed. Thuy rushed for the trees in the opposite direction. A spray of water churned up over his head as he ran. It made it difficult to see the trees, but the dark outline of them was visible.

At the moment of plunging into the woods Thuy looked back. He fully expected the American to be right behind him, but instead he saw nothing. Panting heavily, he pulled his rifle around. He knew he could not now be seen. Where was that guy? Then he saw him standing beside the plane. The American had only made a feeble attempt to come after him. And he had not even fired his weapon. Realizing suddenly that he was likely now to be in the gun sights of the Vietnamese, the pilot scrambled back into the cab of the plane. Thuy held fire as well, being unsure of the presence of American patrols, though he thought it unlikely. It was not his mission at present to kill the enemy but rather to spy on him and bring back information. All in all, the two made a peaceful parting. The gung ho American and the dedicated young guerrilla fighter had met face to face in deadly enmity and neither had fired a shot.

The American, once airborne, circled a few times and, seeing nothing more, climbed up into the sky and disappeared. As soon as he did so, Thuy got out of the area. He knew the pilot might yet call in that artillery strike. And he did. Just a few rounds, for the American was sure Thuy had already gotten away. The shells carried a variable timing device and exploded just above the treetops. They left puffs of black smoke as they showered thousands of needles into the woods. Thuy watched from another patch of jungle several hundred yards away.

It was quite urgent that he do something with his rifle now that he was close to his destination. He must pass for an ordinary peasant. With this thought in mind, Thuy sought out an infertile ravine where there were no cultivated fields or hamlets. He crossed through an open area overgrown with elephant grass that came up to his shoulders. It reminded him of the corn fields his family worked and of the elephant grass they sometimes gathered for use as fuel and a kind of rough fodder. It felt good to be in his own element alone. He was always at home in the jungle. Several crows circled over him cawing. This he did not like. After all, Americans could be lying in wait. On the other hand, they might think it was a tiger or a water buffalo. He climbed one side of the ravine and passed through a grove of banana trees. The large fanlike leaves reminded him happily of the rice balls his mother would wrap up in such leaves for his father, sister and him to take to the rice fields for a day's work. During the transplanting and the harvest, all four of them usually worked in the fields together beneath the hot sun. Then in the heat of day, they would retire to the shade of a tree line to eat their rice balls, their corn cakes, their small portions of meat left over from a ritual slaughter.

Thuy thought about Lan and wondered how his sister was doing. She, of course, would have long since known of the cause of his sudden disappearance. Would she worry? They had been close when they were younger, and there was still a sense of togetherness though the respectable yearnings of adolescence had put some temporary distance between them. And his father. Was he yet alive? Perhaps his mother even now placed a small offering beside the altar in the house for him. There would be many long silences between the two women if both the men were gone now. Village life required many strong hands. But some day the imperialists would be gone. There would be no foreigners, and the people would be in possession of the land they worked. Life would be better for everyone then.

Thuy entered a dense grove of bamboo. The trees grew so close together, one could hardly move between them, and they were covered with a fine razorlike hair that cut stingingly into Thuy's flesh. Here he stashed his rifle, wrapping it in a banana leaf he had cut, then burying it under dirt and forest litter. No one, if anyone like the Americans or South Vietnamese Army troops should happen to enter this ravine, would ever look here. Even most Vietnamese would not remember just where the rifle had been hidden in all that sameness of brush and jungle, but Thuy would. There was a pulse, a rhythm in the natural world, that flowed together with the movements of his own soul. He could find the rifle again. Had not the Venerable Ancient, Lao-tse, once said that beyond the ebb and flow of this world, in transcendent oneness and peace, lay the universal centeredness of one's soul? A man, who in quietness of spirit put his thoughts to rest, need never doubt in his understanding. Without direction or elaborate plans necessary for the blindness of men, Thuy would retrace his steps to this exact spot.

The village of Dai Loc lay along a dusty road known to the Americans as Route Fourteen. This road, such as it was, linked up with another one which ran the whole length of South Vietnam. That made it very important to the Americans in their absurd strategy, or so Duc Thuy thought, for this was Anh Thuy's opinion also. "The Americans," he had observed, "have a foolish predilection for sticking to the main travel routes. This is because they are so reliant on heavy equipment like tanks and trucks, which cannot get about in jungle and bush country like men on foot. So they defend roads like Route Fourteen or Route One along the coast and send out occasional patrols or conduct larger scale operations in the back country. This makes it easy for us. We are able to control most of the countryside and move about freely, mining the roads and hitting their outposts at night. Most of their compounds and outposts are on the roads themselves. Take the one at Dai Loc. As you will see, it used to be a French fort. There is not much left of the fort, just a concrete bunker for their battalion headquarters. The bunker is on a hill. They hold the hill because it is high ground, more easily defended, and because Route Five joins Route Fourteen inside the compound. Anyone passing from one road to the other must go through that place."

Quoc Duong Li was a man in his fifties, a village elder with the lined face, knowing eyes and wispy goatee characteristic of such men. Generally thought of as the "wise ones," these older men had often seen much, for life in the fields was hard and war had been as common a burden of daily life as the dreaded malaria carrying mosquitoes were—for as long as most people could remember. Duong Li had tuberculosis. This was also a common affliction among peasants with their exposed life in the more heavily populated areas.

Thuy found Li sitting in front of his hut in the midday heat. There was a tiny bit of shade there and, that being a good place from which to observe the lively goings-on of the weekly market held in the midst of the adjacent street, he was content to remain and ruminate. These villagers did not work as hard as some others, for the Americans supplied them with rice to keep them "friendly." The rice was distributed under the auspices of the "District Chief," a South Vietnamese government official who had long been suspected by the Americans of selling part of it to the local Viet Cong. For this reason the District Chief was at odds with the South Vietnamese Regional Forces military officer also assigned to the district headquarters. For the latter often pressured the Americans to exert influence on the Saigon government to get rid of the corrupt official. But the Americans did not wish to disturb the peaceful status quo in the area, which they believed the District Chief had purchased from the Viet Cong. Besides, they considered any attempt at eradicating corruption rather futile. It seemed all pervasive to them in a country they did not understand. The battalion commander, a Lieutenant Colonel Watkins, preferred to concentrate on the more vital strategy of carrying out distant operations to clear strategic areas of Viet Cong control. Thus the Americans lived with the Viet Cong under their very nose and fought them in far off places.

Market day was held in the morning. So at noon it was beginning to clear out. But a few betel nut chewing women, with their red gums and black teeth, rattled and jabbered over fluctuating prices and village gossip, as other people stood over them, where they squatted on the dusty road with their wares, and inspected the goods. Just as Thuy arrived a tank rolled through. It came at a good clip, and it was all the villagers could do to get out of the way in time, upsetting their produce and chickens into the roadside ditches. The tank was completely enveloped in a huge cloud of swirling yellow dust. On top of it sat a squad of American infantry, bristling with weapons and bandoleers of ammunition. After it passed, Thuy crossed the road and presented himself to Duong Li. Duong Li did not seem at all surprised to learn of his purpose, for he already knew of the pending attack.

"Welcome, young brother," he said, smiling between his few teeth. "I am delighted to be of assistance." Noting Thuy's interest in the commotion created by the tank, he added, "Do not concern yourself with them. They are used to it. You see even now they have taken up their buying and selling positions on the road again. They will not be long disturbed. The Americans themselves, it seems, have a rule that their vehicles are to proceed slowly through the villages to observe the safety of the people. But it is the mad rush of youth," he said grinning ironically.

V

During Thuy's stay in the village, he observed several things. One was that the village contained a large number of refugees. They had come from other villages which the Americans had burned as suspected Viet Cong strongholds. They were, of course, heavily reliant on the weekly dole of rice parceled out by the District Chief, that portion of the rice, at least, which was not sold to the Viet Cong. The local Viet Cong unit which took the rice in exchange for leaving the district headquarters unmolested turned out, as Thuy learned, to be the sapper unit he had been informed about. This very unit was the one which would approach the battalion at night and fire upon it, drawing return fire into the village they were supposed to leave alone. However, these probing engagements were not exceedingly damaging, killing only a villager or two now and then if they were too slow in rolling into their bunker holes when the shooting started, or if they were unfortunate enough for their hut to take a direct hit from a mortar round. The Americans took the probing actions as a matter of course in war, getting alarmed only if they became too frequent, and the South Vietnamese District Chief felt that not having his own headquarters attacked was sufficient recompense for his efforts. Even the Viet Cong were happy, for they knew that, however passive or docile seeming, the villagers would not learn to love foreign troops who killed them off one by one. Most importantly, the local sapper unit had been able to obtain valuable information as a result of these probes.

Another thing Thuy observed was that the Americans were very nervous about their wooden bridge. The bridge crossed a wide, muddy river, the Song Thu Bon, that separated the Marine compound on its hilltop from the village on the plain below. It served as the connection to Route Five. At all hours of day and night, one or several guards were at work on the bridge firing into the water. They shot at anything they spotted moving toward the bridge with the current either on or beneath the surface of the water. Once during his week's sojourn in the area Thuy saw a local youth leap into the river for a swim early one morning and promptly take a bullet in the shoulder. He was carried into the battalion compound and treated by the Americans.

One morning Thuy showed up at the guard post at the foot of the hill on Route Fourteen leading up into the Marine compound. The sentry, a nineteen year old with carrot red hair and freckles that fascinated the local villagers, was being swamped by a flock of eight or ten boys, ranging in age from five to eleven. This was a normal occurrence, as the boys had no schooling on a regular basis and they did not have to help much at chores, both circumstances being due to the disruptions of war. They spent much of their time hanging around the sentries, begging candy and cigarettes.

As Thuy approached the guard post in the company of an old woman, he heard the boys arguing with the guard. He saw that they spoke some English but he could not understand a word of it. Both Thuy and the old woman were carrying bamboo poles slung over their shoulders and balanced on either end with a heavy load of baskets. The old woman was stooped, slow and wrinkled, but her pace was as steady as that of a water buffalo working in the fields. As the buffalo ambles along with its head down and great horns tilted forward, so she trudged up the road barefoot, head stooped and her burden of pole and baskets bristling forward.

Arriving at the guard post, Thuy looked straight at the Marine, pointed up the road into the compound, and asked quietly in Vietnamese if he and the woman might pass through. The sentry knew almost no Vietnamese, but the youth's meaning was clear. Badgered even then by the bevy of boys surrounding him, he shook them off, as it were, and indicated firmly with gestures and words that Thuy and the woman could not go any further. At that point the old woman repeated Thuy's request, the guard refused, and an argument ensued. The little, bowed over, old woman came alive with argumentative intensity. The guard became somewhat flustered but steadfastly refused. Thuy and the old woman both insisted, hurling incomprehensible Vietnamese at him. At this point the village boys began to serve as translators. Between them all they knew a fair amount of English, gathered from the habit of hanging around the American guards.

"She want to pass," one of them said.

"I know that," the guard answered, "but she cannot."

"She insist."

"Well, tell her she will not be allowed to pass."

One of the boys translated. The old woman answered him in querulous tones. The boy translated into English, "She say she and this man (pointing to Thuy) must go to far away village, can pass only this way."

The guard looked at the old woman. She looked back with dark eyes that seemed, like black wells, to have an infinite, liquid depth. A veritable groan, he thought, seemed to emanate from them, though she was now silent beneath her burden. The guard sighed. "I am going to get hung for this," he said. "Tell them to walk straight through," he said to the boy who was doing most of the translating. "Tell them if they get off this road they will be shot. Ban sung! Shot! You understand?" he repeated, looking at Thuy and the woman and gesticulating with his rifle. Then he saw a Marine approaching him along the dirt road leading down to the guard post. "John!" he called out to him. The man was his relief on duty. When John reached him, he asked him to conduct them through. John agreed and began trudging back up the road with the pair in tow. The red haired guard watched them go, feeling a great sense of relief and congratulating himself on his last minute sagacity and good fortune.

Thuy's eyes were like camera shutters, cautious but missing nothing. The old woman looked about too, being able to do so with a casualness that was denied to Thuy, since she seemed harmless and merely curious. Still Thuy missed nothing, and they would compare notes later. The Marine accompanying them trudged ahead a ways in his impatience, for they were interminably slow, plodding along beneath their burdens, which they had apparently transported in this manner for many a mile already. Though Thuy had been in the area, it was not likely he would be specifically singled out for recognition. He had been careful to attract no undue attention and, barring such special notice, all Vietnamese looked alike to the Americans.

They had not gone far when the Marine's good breeding got the better of him. He took the old woman's burden and was surprised at the weight of it. The sharp ridges of the split bamboo pole cut deeply into his shoulder, and he grimaced to suppress his pain and amazement. The old woman took advantage of the arrangement to look about even more freely.

A group of three Marines they passed looked at them with curiosity, as it was not usual procedure for strange Vietnamese to pass through the compound in this manner, though several local villagers, who had been carefully checked out by the authorities in Da Nang, worked at the battalion mess hall. Most men they passed simply ignored them.

Thuy observed the mess hall on a slight rise of ground to his right. A direct hit on that with a rocket or mortars at the appropriate moment would produce a fair number of casualties. A little further on he observed the motor pool. There were three trucks and several jeeps parked next to a wooden frame hut covered with canvas. Buildings such as this were referred to as "hooches" by the Marines. They lived and worked in them. On the other side of the hut an ontos was parked. Thuy had never seen or heard of an ontos, but it was not difficult to make out what the six big guns were for. The guns were bound together in an L, three on each side, like barrels of a shotgun; could be moved up and down all together; and were capable of firing point blank, singly or in unison, on massed troops. The guns were recoilless rifles that discharged one hundred six millimeter rounds, and the vehicle moved on tracks like a tank, enabling it to get about in the deep, sucking mud of the winter season. Further up, at the crest of the hill, Thuy came upon a row of hooches on his left. These served the men as offices for the battalion headquarters. Adjacent to them and to Thuy's right were several more rows of identical hooches, which served as sleeping quarters. Some of these had their canvas sides rolled up to let in the fresh air, and Thuy could see the rows of canvas cots.

Behind him just a few yards and also to his right, he had made what he thought was the most important observation of all: the location of the ammo dump. A number of small caverns the height of a man, about five feet wide and ten or twelve feet deep, had been dug into the ground. They were supported by rough wooden beams and were lined up in two opposing rows facing into a deep trench. The heavy wooden doors on one of them were swung open, and Thuy could see that it was loaded with cases of ammunition. During an assault, many of these doors would be open as the Marines retrieved ammunition to resupply the men fighting at the perimeter. One lucky hit with a mortar and good-bye Marine compound. At the moment Thuy was making these observations several Marines were busy about the dump, filling sandbags and using them to reinforce the roofs and doors of the open cavern. Two of them had taken off their green fatigue shirts, a white man and a black man. It seemed to Thuy that these Americans ran to extremes of coloration and were as bright and full of contrast as holiday banners.

From the top of the hill, Thuy could clearly observe the adjoining rise of ground upon which was perched the monolithic structure of the mess hall. He could now see that on the other side of it were several big guns. These Americans did have the supporting artillery Duong Li had himself observed. Perhaps they were the very ones which had provided the fire mission for the gung ho spotter plane pilot.

The Marine who was accompanying them brought Thuy and the old woman to the farther guard post, the one which led across the wooden bridge to Route Five. The guards on the bridge looked at the Marine as if he was crazy but made no comment. One of them was firing into the water against the flow of the current. The Marine with Thuy and the woman unburdened himself, returning his load to the woman, who took it calmly and trudged across the bridge with seemingly little effort. He watched them go, beads of sweat gathered on his forehead. He would long recall the cutting weight of that bamboo pole.

Thuy's return trip was a joyous one. He was back in the pleasant green of the tangled forest, which enshrouded him like a mist. He was mist himself, disappearing like a phantom into the green sea of his natural element. The rifle remained untouched where he had left it. The banana leaf it was wrapped in and the light film of cosmoline jelly still coating the metal parts had protected it well. There was no rust. The barrel was cool from lying buried in the earth. He laid it against his hot clammy face. It felt good in the heat of midday.

VI

On leaving the American compound on the bridge side, Thuy had taken stock of the wire. There was an abutment of high ground that extended out toward the river just beyond the point where they had turned off to descend along the road to the bridge. Several sandbag bunkers were spread out along the perimeter where this finger of land joined the hill, and the barbed concertina wire running in rusty rolls between two of them appeared to be broken or down in some way. It would be an easy point at which to penetrate the battalion defenses if, while under the automatic rifle and machine gun fire that would inevitably pour down on them from the bunkers, troops could manage to get up the steep, exposed incline leading to it. Most likely the Marines had claymore antipersonnel mines set up in the gap too. These could be detonated automatically from inside one of the bunkers. Breaching this point would be a job for sappers. They would have to blow up the bunkers to clear the way.

Also Thuy had taken note of the concrete bunker the French had built as a fort overlooking the river. It lay directly behind the huts used as field offices. It housed only the intelligence and tactical command sections of the battalion as well as the center for directing artillery and counter mortar fire (that is, the center that could pinpoint the origins of incoming mortars and direct fire against them). But Thuy did not know this. He simply observed that the flat top of the bunker was bordered by an eighteen inch, concrete parapet. This was a low wall which infantry could lie behind while shooting into the river valley. All this Thuy reported to Anh Thuy and Ngoc Loan when he got back to his company. He had learned of their precise location from another company he ran into. The separate companies kept in touch, sometimes by radio, mostly by messenger, and knew of each other's movements.

Not more than a week later, Thuy was given charge of a rice resupply mission. In truth, he had not been expected to return with so much information, and his success greatly impressed his leaders. It was unusual for someone quite so young to be given such responsibility, but war fought under such primitive circumstances was indeed a meritocracy.

Thuy took two other men with him. They made their way back into American held territory along a portion of the route Thuy had just used, but they did not go as far. The hamlet they came to was neither friendly toward Americans nor insurgents. Neither did it blow with the winds of conquest and reconquest. It wished to be left alone to tend to its farming. But this was war, and it was a village with some of the richest rice harvests in the area. For several years now the Viet Cong had been taking a good portion of that rice for its own resupply. The villagers complied in silence. It was useless to argue. A neighboring hamlet of similar sympathies had felt strong enough to resist, and one morning the village had been mortared, killing a number of people and wounding many others. Thuy knew of this incident. It had not involved his unit but another one fighting in the same cause. The attack on civilians was not a pleasant thing to contemplate, so Thuy never dwelt on it. He understood the inevitable cruelties of war. Such was the inexorable turning of the wheel of life: there was much pain. Anh Thuy, in mentioning the incident once when they were together, had referred to the unfortunate villagers as "reactionary."

The two men with Thuy were much older, one in his middle, the other in his later twenties. But they did not question Thuy's authority. Such authority carried responsibility, and Thuy would have to answer for their success or failure in performance. Better to simply do one's job well and not concern oneself with the triviality of precedence in command.

They came into the village at about midnight. Going straight to the hut of the village chief, they coaxed him outside and, in somewhat heated but muffled tones, discussed their mission with him. This particular village elder was known to be a recalcitrant fellow but he would cooperate in the end. Thuy and his companions learned which hut the surplus from the recent harvest was stored in. All had been prepared beforehand, for the villagers knew of their coming. What the village elder seemed to object to now was Thuy's demand for porters. They were going to take all the rice at once, so the extra carriers were needed. The elder tried to point out that the people worked hard and needed sleep. It was a futile argument. By two o'clock a dozen porters were loaded down with bags of rice and ready to travel. They would not be back until the following night, since a group like that attempting to return in the daylight would create suspicion in any American patrol which might encounter them.

Thuy walked ahead of the porters. His two companions followed somewhat toward the rear of the column on either side of it. The moon was full and the dark silhouettes of the black pajama clad peasants stood out in the shadowy fields. They were rounding a bend along the edge of a rice paddy near a grove of trees when the trouble hit. From across the field against another patch of jungle there was a burst of light: the muzzle flashes of an automatic weapon. As soon as the first shots were fired, Thuy and his companions hit the ground. The guerrilla on the side closest to the ambush had been struck in the head and lay face down in the dark paddy water, his rifle beside him. The villagers—those who had not fallen in the first burst of fire—had dropped their loads and were running wildly in every direction. The fire from the opposing tree line fanned out, cutting them down one by one. In the confusion Thuy and his remaining comrade plunged into the copse of trees nearest them. From inside the woods they shot at the Americans, then found themselves pinned face flat in a waterlogged depression of ground as the machine gun returned to rake the tree line. The water was cold and unpleasant. Bullets thudded into the trees and whistled faintly through the air. When the firing stopped, there was a sudden stillness. Throughout the attack there had been an unearthly silence, as the panicked villagers had scattered and fallen almost without a word.

Thuy lay frozen in place for several long moments. Then he heard a hushed exchange of voices. He lifted his head and looked through the dense tangle of brush and trees. In the moonlight he could see two men standing over the body of a peasant. This particular villager had run straight toward the Marines in his panic. He lay on his back in the bright moonlight dimpled water. So many bullets had hit his chest he was almost cut in half. His arms and legs were strangely twisted, the man being dead before he hit the ground. One leg was folded up under him. His open eyes stared at the sky as though in surprise. Thuy could not make out all these details, but they seemed to be of more than casual interest to the two Marines. Behind them, others had gotten up and were beginning to move off in a single file. They did not even pause to inspect the damage. The two curious Marines joined them, and the patrol disappeared around the trees into another field.

Thuy and his comrade waited some time before getting up. Neither of them had been wounded. Together they dragged their less fortunate companion into a dense tangle of bush further off and concealed the body beneath debris. Later someone would return to bury him, so the Americans would never find him. If possible, fellow villagers would come to bury the porters as well. They would all be placed in a mass grave, since the work had to be done quickly to avoid detection. Even the reluctant villagers would not want the Americans to know that these porters had come from their village. Thuy and his companion carried as much rice as they could between them, along with the extra rifle, and made the long trip through the night back to their company. They did not even pause to let the villagers know what had happened. Such backtracking would be dangerous and without sufficient purpose. They would know soon enough. The ambush had occurred not far away, and the villagers could hear it and see the stray tracer bullets arcing through the sky.

Anh Thuy was gone from his company for a week. He had left his unit the same night Duc Thuy had gone on the resupply mission, so he was not there when Thuy returned. Thuy reported to Ngoc Loan, the company commander, describing in detail everything he could remember. Ngoc Loan nodded but did not elaborate on his thoughts. Obviously, the rice still needed to be collected. Once the winter rains came, his company would move into position for the planned assault. The cold rains got rid of the troublesome ambush patrols and gave freer movement to the Viet Cong.

Right now Anh Thuy was making arrangements for the coordinated assault. Armed with the information Duc Thuy had brought back from the previous mission, he was at a gathering of local party cadres, exchanging intelligence and planning the general outline of battle. In this manner a rough picture was assembled. Little less than a dozen small companies would come together in battalions of three to form into a unit, which the Americans would later refer to as the Rl44th NVA regiment. It was thought to be a North Vietnamese Army regiment because a few of the companies involved were from the North. But most were from the South. The Northerners, however, played a disproportionate role in determining strategy. They worked this out through the party cadres. The position Ngoc Loan's company would take in the upcoming assault would be decided by them. But, as he had first hand knowledge of circumstances at the enemy base camp, Anh Thuy was able to secure tactical responsibility for the section of the Marine battalion perimeter that Duc Thuy had observed to be in bad repair. When Anh Thuy informed the company commander of this upon his return, the latter was visibly pleased.

VII

Word came not long after that Duc Thuy's village had been shelled. It was an American harassment and interdiction fire mission. The random selection process for such missions had finally reached Thuy's village. Word of it came as it always does in the smoldering, leafy green country of Vietnam. It drifted in one morning and settled about Thuy's company like a chilling dew. There were a number of men in that company who were from this village, yet there was no clear knowledge of what had happened, how many casualties or who. The news bearer was a peasant woman from a nearby village. Like many of the communist sympathizers, she helped to form a grassroots intelligence network, by means of which important information was fed to guerrilla units operating nearby. Word was passed willy-nilly from hamlet to hamlet but, though lacking in much specific detail, it was never as weak as mere rumor. Its purpose was the honest reportage of fact and incident.

Not long after this the winter monsoon rains arrived. And this was shortly followed by a flood. As soon as the dark, cloud embroiled winter season had begun, the average temperature dropped nearly thirty degrees: from the high nineties to the low seventies. The ever-present humidity made this difference felt. Thuy and his comrades shivered in their assorted, mismatched khakis and peasant's pajamas. Only a few of them had plastic ponchos to keep them dry. The rest, including Thuy, made out as best they could with straw thatch woven coats and makeshift banana leaf raingear. They were often soaked, slogging through the jungle from camp to camp in bone-chilled misery. Even in the dense forest, the rain, coming down in buckets from a roiling, burst ocean of sky, like the more frequent but warmer summer torrents, streamed off the trees and their leaves in virtual waterfalls. Open roads in the rice paddy country were now sucking sewers of mud. Only the tracked vehicles of the Marines could move about with relative ease in the red slime, and they often got stuck.

This universal misery, however, was an overall advantage to the Viet Cong. Difficult as it might be, movement on foot was at least possible and fairly dependable. The Americans rarely went anywhere, even on foot, without the assurance of vehicular or helicopter support. Now the helicopters were heavily engaged in resupply, trucks no longer being of as much use. So very few troops could be moved. Reconnaissance patrols were the only ones regularly set out in this weather. They kept track of enemy movements and harassed them whenever possible by calling in artillery fire missions on them, while the rest of the Americans remained stymied in their compounds.

This was a time of increased Viet Cong activity, and the inexorable gears of the upcoming assault were to be set in motion. But something else intervened. It was the shadow of worldly appearances, which from time immemorial had kept men in their place by surprising and frustrating them. Now it brought them the aforementioned typhoon. Winds came roaring through the jungle, tearing off branches and carrying sheets of rain. They had risen suddenly from an eerie stillness late at night and had reached peak intensity within the hour. In the space of this time, Thuy and his comrades, who had been caught in the open, as there were no base camps in the vicinity, moved up onto a hillside on the leeward slope. They kept this relatively high ground below the crest for the rest of the night and were nevertheless battered unceasingly. Thuy's straw coat was pulled and whipped about by the winds till it fell apart. He clutched a piece of it and drew it around him, hugging the forest floor. That too was eventually taken away, and he lay there in a ball soaking wet. At one point he heard a groan in the darkness. It was the man next to him, who was in a similar condition. By morning the sun was out.

The storm had served to clear the sky of its load of clouds. It was the first brilliant sunshine they had seen in weeks and, penetrating windfalls or breaks between some of the trees as it did in white and yellow shafts of dizzying light, it set the whole forest ablaze with a cacophony of sounds. Jewel thrushes whistled loudly, and blue flycatchers darted about in the upper branches, as a troop of black gibbons swung noisily past the men through the lower ones. Thuy and his companions did not have to travel far to get to a cleared field, so they broke into it and walked along in the open air to dry off. It was here they noticed that the water in the rice paddies was several feet deep. It rose slowly during the day to about three and a half feet. Eventually word came via the people's grapevine that the Americans were in serious trouble. The flood waters were much deeper around the Marine battalion command post Thuy had reconnoitered. They rose in that vicinity to about five feet, as they were situated in a broad plain punctuated by a few areas of high ground. The command post was itself located in a position high and dry, being on its river side about thirty-five feet above the normal water flow. But its bridge was gone, having been knocked out by a separate wooden bridge that had come with the swollen river current from another American position upstream. This meant that the Marines were effectively cut off from Route Five. Of course, they were cut off on all sides until the water subsided. At the moment, the river channel could not even be distinguished. But the bridge would not be replaced until several days or a week after the water went down.

Meanwhile, the Americans had taken about thirty of the unfortunate local villagers into their compound, where they kept them isolated, dry and under careful guard. They treated the sick among them, but most villagers preferred to take their own risks and simply camped on whatever bits of unoccupied high ground they could find nearest to their drowned homes. When the lowering waters reached the road level, the village men got out their nets and fished for freshwater shrimp and whatever else they could catch in the flooded paddies. All in all, it was a peaceful time, the war having come to a temporary halt in the natural emergency. The Marines sat tight and were resupplied by air. The Viet Cong modified their schedules for the upcoming campaigns. To a peasant farmer, standing in awe before the mysterious ways of both man and the all-pervading Spirit, every event has its trials and compensations.

Ngoc Loan, in conference with Anh Thuy, came to the conclusion that there would be a delay of several weeks in their operations. They decided to return to the vicinity of Duc Thuy's village for a short stay. This would revive the spirits of the men, many of whom were recruited from hamlets in that area and had heard of the recent shelling of the village. There was also a regimental base camp there, and the wooden barracks and better quality food would restore physical strength. When word of this temporary change of plans reached Duc Thuy, he was overjoyed. More than once, thoughts of desertion and going home had crossed his mind after he had learned the disastrous news of the American attack. But he had remained faithful to duty, waiting patiently and quietly, never breathing a word of his anxiety even to his close friend, Anh Thuy. But the party cadre knew what lay in the younger man's heart. For he had known fear and grief himself. When he told Duc Thuy the good news, he commented ironically, "Now a man may return to care for his sibling and parents with the help of his comrades and not alone."

The regimental base camp was a wonderful thing with its wooden barracks and dry hammocks. The thirty-odd men— they had picked up a few recruits in the valley—were all crammed into a single building, and it was hot and muggy in the spate of warmer days that followed the storm. But by the time Thuy and his companions had arrived, the cooler weather was once again on its way, and they did not have to suffer long. They kept their few belongings and combat gear, including weapons, stacked neatly along the walls, which were constructed of wood and bamboo up to the level of a man's waist. Above that were open window bays that let in the cooler air and dim light of the forest, for they were hidden deep in the jungle, where neither American patrols nor aircraft were likely to spot them. Above the windows was a sloping roof that extended out over the windows for protection from the elements. It was laid out in a close grid work of bamboo poles which supported the weight of a thick matting of river palm leaf thatch, which was lashed to them.

Thuy had not seen this camp in many months and had passed through it only briefly at the time of his recruitment. He reveled in the luxury of life under shelter above ground. The people's army was on furlough, a time of increased indoctrination and "discussion," in which individuals were encouraged to air their grievances in the presence of their leaders and comrades. During one such airing of views, Duc Thuy was accused by his erstwhile companion on the rice hauling mission of being responsible for their walking into the ambush. Ngoc Loan intervened and pointed out that such unfortunate events often resulted from the hazards of these missions and that ordinary men could not be expected to see like owls in the dark.

"The moon was in its fullness," Thuy's accuser pointed out. "Brother Thuy was in the lead, at the head of the column. He should have seen the American Marines. It was his duty."

"The Americans were well concealed in the shadows of the opposing tree line," Thuy said. "I looked carefully all about but did not see anything. There was no movement among them, until they opened fire on us."

"Yes," Ngoc Loan observed reflectively, "the American Marines are like tigers with their night ambushes. It is their favorite weapon. But wars are not won by mere ambushes."

"They are carried to victory in the hearts of the people," Anh Thuy observed. He had been quietly watching the younger Thuy's reactions to his accuser. He was pleased to note that the young man had not become flustered but had responded clearly and simply. The Party had great need for such men.

"Let us not dispute the matter further," Ngoc Loan said. "It is a great misfortune that we have lost a loyal comrade, but these things cannot always be avoided in time of war."

Thuy's accuser quietly accepted this decision, for he did not wish to dispute with his commander and had, at any rate, no real evidence to support his concern.

The men ate in small groups, their rice prepared separately in large quantities then distributed to them. All cooking was done during hours of darkness, so that American aircraft flying above the jungle could not spot any smoke. It was also accomplished beneath an open, metal roofed structure, the principal purpose of which, besides offering some protection from rain and falling debris from the trees, was to ward off infrared radar detection from passing aircraft. At the slightest hint of any suspicious sign anyway, the fire was immediately doused.

Such were conditions for the people's fighters at the regimental camp. There were no decadent luxuries or satisfactions for undisciplined desires, such as loose women, but the pace of life was relaxed and comradery ran especially high during such intervals of rest. Men often spoke of the future when all foreigners would be gone from Vietnamese soil and oppressive regimes with their exploiting landlord, city-dwelling retainers would no longer find support in a frightened people. This was worth all the hardship: a glorious future. Anh Thuy greatly encouraged such talk through the content of his daily discussion meetings with the men of his company.

They were the only company quartered in the regimental camp at this time, but there was room for more. A permanent staff of young nurses dressed old wounds which had been inadequately cared for under the makeshift medical aid conditions of field duty. Also a small command and planning staff of men ran the camp. They kept in touch both with the North and with units in the field, mostly by messenger. It was the safest way. As any guerrilla fighter knows, intelligence security, fluid movement, and flexible communication are essential ingredients of success in insurgent warfare. These interests are best served by simplicity of means; therefore the unsophisticated fighting equipment of the people's army was, in fact, a great boon. It helped to offset the American superiority in hardware and control of the air. "A duty of the people's army," Anh Thuy once told the men, "is to make the great American military machine feel the weight of its own encumbrance. We must turn their superiority of equipment and weapons against them. This," he pointed out, "is why we carry mortars for fire support and use artillery only where the big guns can be kept across the border and out of their reach."

The American prisoners being held in the camp were a surprise to young Thuy. There had not been any present when he was in the camp before. Now there were three awaiting transfer to more permanent facilities across the border in Laos. These three Americans had been captured at once by the same Viet Cong unit. They had, Anh Thuy had discovered and related to him, simply been stopped on a road while traveling in a jeep. The jeep had hit a small mine which had blown off a wheel but had not overturned the vehicle or injured the men, as the metal floor of the jeep was heavily sandbagged. When the jeep had scooted to the side of the road and stopped in a ditch, six Viet Cong walked out of the surrounding jungle, rifles leveled. The Marines never had a chance to lift their weapons.

The three men were kept in separate holding pens. These pens were bamboo cages which were about seven feet wide and seven feet deep and not quite tall enough to stand up in. The men, grown thin from a month's unvarying ration of plain boiled rice and water, stared sullenly at onlookers from deep sockets. Such food would easily sustain a Vietnamese peasant but not the Americans. They were inured to comparatively rich fare. Even their bulky, somewhat monotonous "C rations," supplied by truck and air, seemed shockingly rich in variety to a people's soldier, who carried a week's ration of rice in a bag tied about his waist. These Americans seemed like over-fed bulls, equipped with horns too heavy for fighting. Yet they fought well enough when they got the chance, as Thuy himself had begun to learn.

VIII

The planning and command staff at the regimental camp was responsible primarily for organizational, intelligence and large scale resupply purposes, mostly the supply of weapons and ammunition. It was not a field regiment, and, though the parent regiment for Thuy's company, it was not operationally in control of the unit when it was in the field. Such operational link-ups depended on circumstances and battle plans of the moment. It was a warfare of exigencies. Each company was loosely in communication with the others in its present area of operations, but functioned separately and individually in small harassing missions until called together with others for a larger assault. They were like a cloud of summer midges which a man walks into and strikes at with his hands but can neither damage nor disperse at will. At every blow, they dissolve yet remain as a continual torment to him.

After about a week in the camp, Duc Thuy was allowed to return home. What he found made him sick, and for the first time since a small child he felt uncontrollable anger. He was ashamed of his reaction and tried not to appear visibly shaken. His own family had escaped unhurt, but many others in the village had been injured or killed. This arbitrary assault upset him more than the Marine ambush had, for he could think of no reason, no provocation for the artillery attack.

"We were short-handed in bringing in the rice harvest this year," his mother observed. She was squatted by the fire inside the hut, stirring coals in preparation for the heating of rice cakes made up earlier in the day. It was late afternoon. "We could have used your help." She looked up at Thuy. "As you can see, your father is still very ill. The fever left him for awhile, then returned, went away and returned again." Looking down to place the rice cakes, which were wrapped in moist banana leaves, on the coals, she added, "We were not able to bring in all the corn. The birds have eaten well this season, but the bellies of your people are not as full as they were before."

Thuy could see his father lying near the fire on a mat. In the shadows of the enclosed room, he observed that the man was quiet, restful, looking up at him intently. Thuy turned to him. "I am sorry, father, that I did not consult you before going off. It was most disrespectful."

Thuy's father raised himself up on one arm. Thuy's mother turned to help him, but he waved her off. "The chills have passed for now," he reassured her. "I am not disappointed in you, my son," he said. "Your mother is also pleased. Do not let this old woman fool you. She complains much, but in her heart she is proud that you are willing to fight against the Americans."

"It is an evil thing that so many foreigners should come to oppress us," Thuy's mother added. "And kill innocent farmers, and women and children, and bomb our fields, destroy our homes. It is an evil, incomprehensible thing. Have you killed any Americans?" she asked angrily, though her eyes betrayed another emotion.

"It is not good that we should ask such questions," Thuy's father said.

"It is all right," Thuy said. "I have not." His mother gave him a questioning look. "There was an ambush," Thuy went on. "The Americans caught us by surprise when we were transporting rice. The people who were helping us were all killed, and one man from another village near here was lost. A comrade and I were able to escape."

"The Americans should all be killed," his mother said, lifting the steaming rice cakes one by one off the red coals. "Why must they come here to oppress us, to kill our people and our young sons?"

Thuy's sister entered the hut as his mother was speaking. She came over and sat on the side of the fire opposite her father. In the light that entered through the smoke hole in the roof, and also through the doorway, Thuy could make out the youthful face, slender arms. He thought of a water buffalo calf, not more than a month old, which had this look of tender youthfulness about it. "You have been in the fields?" he asked his sister.

"No, I was in the forest gathering shoots. I placed them inside the door, mother." She looked at Thuy. In her mind she was reading the face of her brother. Written upon it were secrets of experience which had begun to lengthen the distance of years between them.

In the evening Thuy walked about the village inspecting the damage. His sister accompanied him. The huts which were destroyed had been rebuilt, and it was difficult to see material evidence of the shelling, other than a crater in the dirt street between the two rows of thatch huts. This street did not lead anywhere. It was simply a clearing. The hole was about a foot and a half deep and three feet in diameter. Thuy's sister took him to a hut which had a family of five. Here he witnessed a strange thing. All the family members—two children and three adults, the father of the children being a cousin of his—had bits of shrapnel in the soles of their feet. On no other part of their bodies had they been injured. "When the bomb went off," Thuy's sister told him, referring to the artillery shell that had struck outside the hut, "they were all asleep inside." She pointed to an adjoining room containing the wooden platforms which served as beds with the sleeping mats rolled up on them. "They were all facing the same way and did not have time to get into the shelter holes." Thuy observed that two of the adults, the children's mother and her mother, had difficulty getting about. "The wounds are deep, and we were not able to remove all the metal," the elder woman told him.

As it was evening just before twilight, the village chickens could be heard squawking and fussing in the nearby trees of the forest, where they were gathering to roost. A brown, lop-eared dog of medium size, which had lain about alternately in the sun and shade all day, was now busily sniffing about the huts. The smell of cooked rice, corn, and fish oil filled the street, and a thin haze of blue smoke hung above the forest, where it had drifted on a breeze from the huts.

Another family Thuy and his sister paid a call to had suffered the loss of two children. One five year old was left, and the old grandmother had been permanently paralyzed down the whole length of one side of her body. She had been struck by shrapnel in the head, and the tiny piece of metal was lodged somewhere in her brain. The shelling had come once, at night, had lasted for several minutes, and had not been repeated since. It was as though it had dropped out of the sky like a late summer cloudburst of rain.

When Thuy returned to his unit after a stay of several days in his village, he went with a greater sense of purpose. His own recent experience and the suffering of his village had personalized the war for him. He still held to his socialist ideals, but he was now a man who was not only liberating his people but defending his family as well. The incident of the recalcitrant village which another Viet Cong unit had mortared did not daunt his conviction, but it did perhaps increase in complexity his sense of justice. He knew that the complications of this world were far too great to be easily understood. But he also knew that one fought for justice simply because the spirit of truth and justice lay within one's heart. A man's life was a region of changeful appearances that could only tire the mind if he attempted to extract meaning from them. But a man's spirit lay in rest, like the heart of the sun, touching all things with its purpose. Where it went forth and what it greened was neither good nor bad but inevitable. Thus truth arose, like young plants, where the energy of this inner life had placed it. A just cause in defense of one's people was no more to be impeded than the spreading morning light.

Word reached Thuy's company that the flood waters had receded. The Americans had begun to repair the damage to their bridges and low lying fortifications. Their patrols had resumed operations in the surrounding countryside. Thus Thuy's whole company, in returning to action, was proceeding along a jungle trail in a loose double column in the hill country they usually occupied, when a Marine reconnaissance patrol spotted them. These reconnaissance men were on a high piece of ground, concealed by dense brush at the forest edge, and they could see Thuy's unit snaking up a gentle slope beside the clearing that separated them from the Marines by a hundred yards. The Marines lay still as impending death on the jungle floor and, in hushed tones, called in an artillery strike. Several minutes passed. The rear end of the Viet Cong column was now exposed. Then they heard the screaming shells, the loud crack and boom of explosions. Only five or six shells came in at first, and they fell short. Thuy's unit was in complete disarray, each man hugging his own piece of ground somewhere to either side of the trail. They did not know where the Americans were, but they realized this was no arbitrary fire mission. Ngoc Loan yelled to the men to get up and move to the other side of the hill they had been traversing. One by one and in twos and threes the guerrillas rushed through the jungle.

The Marines, confident the next fire mission would get the Viet Cong—the Marines were rapidly calling in map coordinate adjustments over the radio—began to shoot at them. This gave away their position. There were only seven men in the reconnaissance team, and they ought not to have risked themselves directly against such odds. The second volley of shells came in with shocking suddenness. Eight or nine rounds impacted directly on the trail and close along either side of it. A few rounds exploded against trees, cracking limbs and sending debris flying. The earth shook repeatedly like a tremor. Nothing seemed stable or fastened down. All the men in the Viet Cong company had gotten away from the trail and the exposed side of the hill. They now lay face down on the verdant smelling jungle floor in whatever little hollow or depression or behind whatever log, rock or trunk they had found.

Thuy, while waiting out the time allotted by the American fire mission for the possibility of a direct hit, thought of his village. He thought of the shells falling there, killing so many because they had not expected it and the shells had come down directly onto the hamlet. Did the Americans know about the hamlet? Was it on their maps? Thuy did not know. He did not know if the attack on his own village had been by chance or direct plan.

While there this time, his company had picked up several new recruits. A young, inexperienced boy his own age was now lying directly behind him in what appeared to be a dry, shallow stream bed. The bed apparently served as a run-off for flood waters, rather than as a regular conduit. It was cool, soft and damp, but not terribly muddy from the recent heavy rains. The boy was clutching Thuy about both ankles. Each time a round shrieked in over the trees, cracked thunderously on impact and boomed, shaking the earth and sending shrapnel whining through the forest, he squeezed Thuy's ankles with all his strength. The pain from this was not inconsiderable, but neither Thuy nor the boy uttered a word.

When the second barrage was over, Thuy could hear Ngoc Loan's voice. He was shouting for the men to regroup about him. Because of the shooting, he had a precise idea of the location of the Americans, and he was not going to miss any opportunities. Quickly taking stock of his gathered forces, he saw that they had sustained no losses or injuries. He sent half of them, about sixteen men including Duc Thuy, toward the Americans under the command of Anh Thuy. The others spread out in the brush to get a clear view of the American position and opened fire. Two of them set up a mortar tube and began lobbing shells up onto the rise where the Marines had been spotted. Anh Thuy's detachment circled about and came up on one side of the hill under cover of the jungle and the protection afforded by this base of fire.

The Marines, however, though foolhardy, were no fools. They knew they were in trouble and had retreated halfway down the back side of the hill before being caught by the Viet

Cong unit. They were thus well out of range of the misdirected mortars but were soon pinned down by a withering spray of small arms fire. They had little protection and could see virtually nothing in the dense brush, for there were many breaks in the forest canopy in this area, the increased access of sunlight making the undergrowth almost impenetrable. As the approaching guerrillas quickly spread out, their rifle fire came from all sides. In minutes one American was dead and another wounded. A Marine was shouting frantically into the radio, and with miraculous quickness the churning of helicopters began to sound over the treetops. But the airmen could not see down through the dense jungle, and the only available clearing was the one near the trail Thuy's company had been traveling on.

The Marines were splayed out in a semicircle, lying on their bellies, the crest of the hill behind them. The wounded man was still firing; the dead Marine had been pulled into the center of the half-circle. As Duc Thuy and his comrades moved forward under Anh Thuy's orders and the cover of heavy fire, Thuy caught glimpses of the American who was still shouting into the radio. Another Marine lay beside him, yelling alternately into the handset then handing it back to resume firing. Thuy, lying now not more than fifty feet away, took careful aim and fired several bullets into the spot where he had seen them. The next time he caught sight of them, he saw that he had struck the radio man, for he was lying there motionless and the other man had taken over the radio. Thuy, who with one or two others was forward of most of his companions, was within thirty feet of the Marines. The mortars had not gone off for several minutes, and he knew that meant Ngoc Loan understood the Americans' new position and situation and was also closing in with his men.

Then another sound was heard, like the roar of one hundred twenty millimeter rockets but even louder. There were Phantom fighter-bomber jets above the jungle, and their dive over the treetops in the glinting sunlight completely obscured the noise of the helicopters. It also signaled massive death. For, because the Americans had no other choice, they had called a napalm bombing strike in practically on top of themselves. In seconds large sections of the jungle were on fire with the burning gel, which clung to branches and tree trunks, draping the green growth like a flaming moss. The heat was intense, the black smoke blinding, and it became difficult to breathe. Immediately, even without orders from Anh Thuy or Ngoc Loan, the Viet Cong soldiers began to withdraw. There is no defense against napalm.

Later, from a considerable distance, Thuy and his comrades heard the helicopters land and take off again. They knew then that the Marines had made it to the clearing. A belated inspection also proved that they had taken their dead and wounded with them. The Viet Cong had suffered no casualties themselves.

IX

Duc Thuy and his company now settled into an area of mixed jungle, rice paddy and dry fields near a village situated along Route Fourteen. The particular stretch of dirt road this hamlet bordered was known as "Liberty Road" to the Americans. Complete liberty from insurgent activity was something this road had never known. The Americans considered the hamlet "friendly" because a good part of its population was composed of refugees, who had been forcibly resettled there by the French. They had long since blended in with the original inhabitants, sharing in the work and produce of the fields—such as there was of it for farming operations carried out on a battleground. These people were always very cordial when any Americans passed through or one or two of the Marines dropped in for food or drink. But their congeniality was a disguise, for they provided vigorous support to the Viet Cong. That is why, to the complete bewilderment of the Americans in their many efforts to clear the area of guerrillas, the road was never safe.

Every morning the Marine mine sweep teams came out, rain or dry, searched for and dug up the mines Thuy and his comrades had planted in the road overnight. In doing so, the Marines took casualties from snipers they never saw. If they beefed up the patrols that accompanied the sweep teams and searched the surrounding countryside on either side of the road, the sniping would stop. But the Marines were spread thinly over the northern provinces of South Vietnam and could not long sustain such expenditures of manpower.

Another index of confusion regarding the Americans was the way they responded to vehicle ambush incidents on the road. Once the mines were cleared, usually by nine o'clock in the morning, Marine vehicles—jeeps, tanks and trucks—in such numbers as the weather would permit, began passing back and forth. If combat activity had been light in the area for awhile, the lighter vehicles—jeeps and trucks—might often travel alone, manned perhaps by just two men: a driver and his "shotgun rider." At such times the general area was designated a "controlled fire zone" by the Marine commander. Marines were then under orders to shoot only when shot at or, of course, if they clearly saw someone armed. But if several ambushes occurred, and especially if there were losses, the Marine lieutenant colonel in command of the unit responsible for securing the area—the officer in control of the very battalion whose command post Thuy had scouted out—would temporarily redesignate the area a "free fire zone." Thence forward, light vehicles were not permitted to travel alone but had to wait at the nearest American compound to form up into convoys. Also anyone on those convoys who spotted anything suspicious was free to open fire at will. Thus, during such periods, the Marines expended an enormous amount of lead. Nothing was safe, including something as large and obvious as a water buffalo. This was not very constructive toward local pacification efforts, as the colonel well knew, so, before long, he would lift the free fire zone designation and reimpose his controlled fire zone orders. It was an endless round of events which kept everyone occupied and accomplished nothing, from the American point of view, at least.

In fact, their frustration was so great that at one point they had completely destroyed another hamlet that had been located along this road and resettled most of its inhabitants elsewhere. There had been so many ambush and mine incidents in the vicinity of this other village, which was conveniently closed in on one side by a patch of jungle, that a Marine flamethrower tank had rolled up one morning and burned it and the adjacent patch of jungle to the ground. Though it had been more than a year since the incident, the area, now thoroughly covered with new growth, still had a charcoal look to it. A patrol had rounded up the frightened villagers, who had scattered into the surrounding rice paddies when the tank began its work.

These Viet Cong phantom tactics did not always affect only Americans or local inhabitants. War spreads like brush fire in such circumstances, burning out here, starting up there. Only recently a bus load of Vietnamese civilians had struck a mine on the road, for the members of Thuy's unit, and of the one which had operated in the same area before it, replanted as many mines as they could as soon as the sweep teams had been through. The mine, a powerful one, had shredded the metal hull of the bus and scattered people, pigs and chickens, or parts of them, all over the adjacent fields.

Another incident of insurgent strike and disappear operations had hit a small American utility truck on its return to the battalion command post from an ammunition run. A sudden spray of bullets from the brush alongside the road had pierced the windshield, immediately killing the shotgun rider and wounding the driver in the neck. Still conscious and breathing, while bleeding profusely from the throat, the young Marine jammed his foot into the gas pedal and raced along on two flattened tires to the command post. He died inside the compound.

During this new period of operations for Thuy's unit, which was relatively slack duty due to the intermittent inclemency of the weather that rendered vehicular traffic impractical at times, a close bond of friendship developed between Duc Thuy and the raw recruit who had clung to his ankles during the shelling. Thuy knew the young man, Vuong Gia Ky, who was his own age and a distant cousin from the same village. At first a little put off by Ky's reaction at the time of the shelling, Thuy gradually warmed to him, as they often spent time together discussing former days at home. In fact, the two became somewhat inseparable, the new recruit clinging to Thuy for a sense of orientation in his yet unfamiliar role. These two both now became close adherents to the philosophy of Anh Thuy. The three were often together during lulls in activity, the two younger men listening intently to the experienced wisdom of the party cadre. Anh Thuy, however, never lost his special regard for Duc Thuy. The calm intelligence and proven courage of the younger man impressed him greatly. Once he had even taken Duc Thuy with him to a general rendezvous of local party cadres. It was clear to all concerned that he was grooming the younger man for just such a role.

One day the three of them, Anh Thuy, Duc Thuy and Gia Ky, took up residence in the hamlet on Liberty Road. It was not an impressive village, being entirely composed of thatch houses and lacking the plastered adobe, red tile roofed structures imposed by the French influence on some other areas, like the Dai Loc district headquarters. Whenever these more durable structures were blended in with the thatch dwellings, usually serving as schools or government buildings, they gave the village a more substantial look. But this hamlet had that temporary appearance a community engaged in its politics might have been expected to have. Yet it had weathered many storms.

The three men took up their residence in separate homes, but the place of real interest was the dwelling Anh Thuy honored with his presence. It was home to a childless couple in their thirties. They were former residents of the hamlet the tank had destroyed and, even before that, had lost their only child to an accident. The four year old girl had found an unexploded mortar round which had fallen sometime months before near the hamlet. While she was sitting on the ground happily playing with it, it went off.

This hut became the location for a new weapons cache for the Viet Cong company. The village was not far from the district headquarters and the Marine battalion command post that was scheduled for the assault, so it was a good pick up and rendezvous point. Here the men could load up with the extra mortar tubes, machine guns and ammunition they would need on that night. Such operations almost always took place at night.

The location was ideal. Being right under the nose of the Americans, they would never be noticed. During evening hours after the sun went down and the Marines had closed the roads—which means they had abandoned them except for their deadly ambush patrols—Thuy and his comrades worked hard to prepare the bunker. In a week a good sized cavern had been opened up beneath the village. Its entrance was inside the hut Anh Thuy had taken up residence in. It was in the inner room of the two room dwelling, and the hole in the dirt floor was covered by a mat and a wooden bed. After having dug it, the three men and their company comrades filled it in a period of three nights. Along with the hardware of war was included a supply of rice already bound up in the small portable bundles that could be carried so easily about a man's waist. Also in one corner was a collection of hollow reeds, all recently gathered and cut to approximately the same length. There were enough to supply one to every man in the company. The reeds might well save the life of a man after a night assault. For when they withdrew, dawn would be fast approaching, and the Marines, like angry bees, would be in hot pursuit at the first morning light. When the Marine patrols struck out in every direction searching for the guerrillas, the people's fighters, many of them, would not have had time to make good their escape. Then the reeds would serve them well as breathing tubes in the river and flooded rice paddies where they hid, alone, one by one. In the days that followed, before they were able to regroup, the rice they carried would support them. More than once already in his travels, Duc Thuy had been forced to eat the stuff raw. Though it had lain in his belly like stones on a river bottom, it had kept him going.

Thuy enjoyed his stay in this village. He was there for several weeks. The Marines often passed through and would stop at times for a bowl of soup or a beer. Then the Vietnamese and Marines would engage in friendly banter, as the Americans considered this a "secured village," though the area seemed to be infested with Viet Cong. Thuy remembered a particularly nervous young Marine who had arrived with a South Vietnamese soldier late one afternoon in the latter's rickety old army truck. They had had some soup, into which the American, a thin, blond man of about twenty, had dumped a hefty load of hot sauce, not knowing what it was. As they talked to each other and the peasant woman who served them, the Marine, his eyes watering profusely, ate his soup under excruciating pain of politeness. Afterwards they stepped back out onto the road, which was where Thuy observed them. The woman later told him about the hot sauce.

As soon as they hit the street, the Marine and his South Vietnamese Army companion began to argue. The South Vietnamese soldier spoke some English, the Marine even less Vietnamese. Nevertheless, they were quite clear in expressing, or stressing, their points of interest. The Vietnamese wanted to leave him and go on to his own company to get there before dark. He insisted that other Americans coming through would pick up the Marine and take him to the battalion compound. Standing beside the truck, the South Vietnamese insisted on his point, then climbed into the driver's seat. The Marine, visibly shaken, placed his right hand on the butt of his holstered pistol, repeating several times in broken Vietnamese that he was not staying behind. Finally, the South Vietnamese soldier relented and they drove off leaving a cloud of dust, as the intermittent rains of the season had not poured for two days, though the sky remained gray.

Apparently, Thuy reflected, the American had been concerned that there might be Viet Cong lurking in the village, who could pop out of the woodwork the minute the South Vietnamese soldier left. Since the latter had family there, he was esteemed by the Marine as a guarantor of safety.

In succeeding days, the drizzling rains reappeared, and Thuy's company got its orders. The Marines, slowed within their compounds by the weather, which made most forms of vehicle transport impossible, were of little effect at this time in policing the surrounding country; so the guerrillas were able to move openly and freely with little caution, even during daylight hours. This greatly augmented resupply operations in preparation for the assault, and the other Viet Cong and North Vietnamese companies which had congregated in the area over the last few weeks made their final preparations.

Then, on a wet, miserable night in November, they began to mass in the village across the river from the Marine compound Duc Thuy had reconnoitered. Thuy's company had been assigned the task of penetrating the breach in the wire Thuy had observed before and which they knew from fresher intelligence still remained unrepaired. Other units would attack other points on the perimeter, the North Vietnamese taking up the center position and scaling the broad, steep slope of the hill that rose above the river. One Viet Cong company was positioned to assault across fairly level but well fortified terrain to the rear of the compound on the side opposite these bluffs. It was not expected that they should penetrate the perimeter. Their mission was to preoccupy a number of troops, drawing them from the other side. They would attack first. Then a mortar barrage would pound the Americans, as the sappers, who now accompanied Thuy's unit, scrambled up and placed their satchel charges against the two bunkers flanking the spot Thuy and his comrades were assigned to assault. This section of the perimeter was approached through a ravine. The massed troops all along the bluffs—having by then slipped across the river individually or in small groups aboard an occasional sampan well upstream from the bridge—would also begin their advance under cover of the mortar barrage, while the Marines, hopefully, still had their heads down.

X

Few Americans have ever understood the oriental mind with its patience and subtlety. The Americans think in big categories and assume that others do so. The Vietnamese slip like a mist through the porous texture of their logic. Thus the Americans think an area secured when it is not, a foe a friend because he is not hostile to one's face, or a friend a foe because his ideas are different. In this manner they habitually overlook the conditions which cause men to think and act in various ways throughout the world.

The massing of enemy troops below the battalion compound that night in early November 1967 had not been expected. Some intelligence of the coming attack had filtered through in bits and pieces from informants in the village of Dai Loc, but the Americans had chosen to disregard it. In their defense, it should be pointed out that much of such information was always coming to them and most of it proved to be thoroughly invalid. In fact, it was Viet Cong agents and sympathizers themselves who manufactured most of the bad information. This helped to discredit those portions of truth which inevitably leaked through. It was a technique which, though understood, generally proved far too subtle in practice for the Americans. They were in a foreign land, an incomprehensible environment of seemingly devious and slippery people, wholly impalpable in their ways. It was a case of building Western style democracy with bricks of sand.

Forming up in the shadows with his company, not far below the downstream side of the bridge, Thuy could nevertheless see some of the movements of the men in the main body. They were massing below that part of the hill on which was located the largest section of the Marine compound and were between it and the river, some fifty yards away at that point. How, Thuy wondered, was it that the bridge guards were not aware. The lone sentry on duty stood out clearly on the wooden structure. His head was bent over as he clutched his M-16 rifle beneath his poncho. The rain, an unusually drenching one for winter, was pouring down in bucket loads and rolled off him in waterfalls. At that very moment two sappers were fixing explosive charges beneath the bridge. They were swimming in the water. The three companions of the sentry were asleep in a small sandbag bunker located at the end of the bridge resting on the bank of the river opposite the Marine compound. When the sappers had finished, they allowed the current to carry them downriver. One of them, as he drifted, strung out a detonator wire. They came ashore next to Thuy and his company.

Thuy glanced across the river's rain broken, heavy flowing surface to the adjacent hamlet. Vietnamese lived on both sides of this river, but the district headquarters was on the side Thuy was on. On the other side, in the quiet and stillness, in the middle of the village street among the unaware, sleeping inhabitants, several mortar tubes were being set up. Closer to the bridge on that side an RPG team of two men aimed their rocket launcher at the bunker containing the three sleeping Marines.

The men in Thuy's company were strung out in two lines near the bottom of the ravine, along either side. The slopes were almost vertical except at the center of the ravine, so it would be difficult for the Marines to fire down on them, especially if they were not sure of where the Viet Cong were in those first crucial moments. For even now the sapper team of five men was ascending the draw. When the shooting started, Thuy and his comrades would provide them with cover fire. This, while the Marines were keeping their heads low, would spare them a few moments for their dash toward the wire and the two bunkers. Then Thuy and his comrades would make their rush up the same draw. Meanwhile, they lay soaking wet, concealed by whatever brush was available. The sappers were entirely naked. It facilitated work among the wire obstacles.

Far from Thuy's point of observation, he knew a company was in place on the level ground on the other side of the battalion compound. He knew they would not rush the perimeter, where the wire emplacements were in good condition, the bunkers close together, the machine guns many and well oiled. But they would lay down a withering volley of fire to draw as many Marines as possible toward them. He knew this company would be the first to open fire, and that that would function as a signal to the mortar crews in the village on the other side of the river to begin lobbing rounds into the Marine compound.

Thuy was impatient. He had difficulty not sliding in the rain sloughing mud, for he was hugging a sloping piece of ground fifteen feet above the ravine floor. Any machine guns in the bunkers above would undoubtedly concentrate their first burst of fire into the center of the draw, he reassured himself, and therefore onto the ravine floor. A little way upstream from the bridge in the sheets of now blowing rain, Thuy could again make out the shadowy movements of the main body of troops. Here the North Vietnamese units were concentrated. They were tough, experienced fighters, having struggled under incessant bombing down the long Ho Chi Minh trail. By the time these men reached the South from their homes in North Vietnam, before ever having laid eyes on an American soldier or Marine, they were hardened combat veterans. Though impossible to make out, Thuy knew they were forming in ranks, or waves, for the main line of assault up the broad face of the hill before them. He glanced back over at the wooden bridge. The sentry, still bent over against the pouring, blowing rain, had not even so much as moved .

The company on the opposite side of the compound waited for the wind to die down. Even without that, it would be hard enough for the advancing troops to get a foothold and keep moving in the deep, slippery, sucking mud. Then they opened fire. The bullets flew in a sheet across the low-strung concertina wire, whining, pattering and thudding into the sandbag bunkers on the perimeter with their heavy wooden struts and beams. This was followed by the mortars, lighting up in short flashes in the compound as they hit. They made a crumping sound, like large hand grenades, when they exploded, but their deadly shrapnel made no sound at all.

The five sappers in the ravine scrambled quickly up the draw as Thuy and his companions fired steadily on the two bunkers. Each line of men aimed at the bunker on the opposing side of the ravine, but even then the angle of fire was ridiculous. The sides of the ravine were too steep. It was incumbent on those sappers to get up there quickly. Thuy saw a flash with his right eye and glanced over at the bridge. The flash had been accompanied by a sharp crack, and Thuy could see that the bunker at the far end of the bridge was destroyed. One side of the wood and sandbag structure was demolished.

As he looked, the bridge went, buckling slightly upward and collapsing into the water. In the flash of this second explosion, Thuy lost sight of the sentry, but he thought he detected his body seconds later in the water.

"Let us go!" he heard. It was Anh Thuy. The men on either side of the ravine got up and started working their way in the slipping mud toward the narrow end of the draw. The Marines were firing from the bunkers above. A red arc of machine gun bullets hit the bottom of the draw and ricocheted like floating coals through the air. The gunner adjusted his aim, and the line of tracers climbed the wall of the ravine in front of Thuy. His instinct was to drop to the ground but he kept moving. He had already seen the sappers retreat down the draw after placing their satchel charges against the bunkers. He saw one of them fall. He knew the bunkers would go. As he scrambled around the bodies of two men who had been felled by the machine gun, the bunkers simultaneously lit up the night.

By this time the Marines had gotten flares up into the night sky. It was two o'clock in the morning and very dark due to the rain. The flares swung in little glowing balls from their parachutes. Men and bushes seemed to blend together and change places in the shifting light. Duc Thuy saw that Anh Thuy was about halfway up the slope at the end of the draw. In front, well ahead of Anh Thuy, were three men. The fighting on this section of the perimeter, in spite of the destruction of the two bunkers, was by no means over, and as the three men neared the wire, he saw one of them double over and drop. The other two advanced several yards, then were back lit by a sudden flash. They were killed by a claymore mine detonated by one of the Marines. Soon Anh Thuy and a half dozen others were at the wire. It was completely down at this point, as Duc

Thuy and later observers had reported. The Marines, in the carelessness of fighting pride, had never repaired it.

Duc Thuy saw Anh Thuy and the others throw themselves down. A machine gun raked over the top of them. Thuy and most of the other men in his company stopped and began firing at the point from which the machine gun bullets were coming. The gun was easy to spot because of the bursts of tracer rounds which were coming from its muzzle in red streaks. Thuy and his comrades had not any of them expended a single bullet during the past several minutes of the rush. Now, the majority of them being almost on line, they provided heavy support. It was enough to break the machine gun's action momentarily. Duc Thuy began to run. His lungs felt raw from hoarse breathing, and his legs ached from hard work in the heavy mud. But in seconds he was up with Anh Thuy, and the two of them reached the wire together. As he leapt easily over the few strands of broken, rusty concertina wire, he saw a white muzzle flash light up the end of a rifle barrel in the ditch immediately in front of him. He felt a slight sting on his left hip. The rain had not abated, but he could make out a pale white face. He put a bullet into the middle of it. As he did, another face rose out of the dark trench before him. A combined expression of fear and determination loomed toward him then fell back. Anh Thuy, who had shot the second Marine, leapt over the trench, turned to his left and sprayed a burst of rounds from his AK-47 automatic rifle down the length of it. Several other comrades, who had crossed the wire right behind them, did the same on the right.

Immediately they fanned out inside the perimeter. A few Marines from further down the line opened fire on them but a team of eight men closed in on and extinguished them. It was now quiet on this finger of land, for it had not been heavily manned, and due to its distance from the main area of the compound, its relative unimportance, and the presence of no sleeping quarters or other facilities there, no other Marines had come to reinforce it during the mortar barrage. This barrage had stopped, and that meant the main body of North Vietnamese and Viet Cong troops had advanced close to the perimeter. It was the duty of Thuy and his comrades to get over there and draw fire off the main line of assault. The run towards that part of the compound was no short distance. Thuy did not even have time to examine his wound, though, since it caused him no disability, he realized it must not be a serious one. Gia Ky, his young friend, ran along beside him, struggling to keep up. He had not been at it as long as Thuy and some of the others.

In the weird, shifting shadows of the flares, they could see Marines darting back and forth. Duc Thuy recognized that these men were running between the ammo dump and the side of the perimeter facing the river. The Marines had by this time long since discovered the principal direction of attack and were doing their best to resupply and reinforce that section of the perimeter. They did not know that the perimeter had been breached at another point.

Several Marines were driving back and forth on little, flat-topped, motor driven "mules," carrying wounded. These light vehicles negotiated the mud with little problem. The rain had let up. The gunfire on the right, riverside perimeter was intense. Elsewhere it was lighter. The battle was coalescing at this point.

It was just as Thuy and several of his comrades, including Gia Ky, were coming into the main area of the compound near the row of office hooches that they were spotted. A Marine on his mule leapt off the vehicle and shot two rounds at them. Both bullets hit Gia Ky. The mule careened on a way on the uneven ground and tipped over, the inert body that was its cargo slipping off into the mud. Gia Ky knelt on the ground. Duc Thuy saw that the bullets had entered his friend's stomach and chest. He put his hand to Gia Ky's shoulder. Gia Ky turned his head toward him, staring dreamily. He tried to focus his eyes. His failure to do this brought an odd smile to his lips. Without uttering a sound he fell over and stopped breathing. This had taken place in perhaps thirty or forty seconds, but it was long enough for the guerrillas to overwhelm the mule driver. Anh Thuy had come up beside Duc Thuy and said quietly, "Our comrades are in need of us." They left Gia Ky where he lay.

Other Marines now came out from behind the row of hooches on their right. As soon as they saw the Viet Cong they started shooting, throwing themselves down in the mud. The rain had picked up again, and it was difficult to see. Their M-16 rifles were equipped with muzzle flash suppressors, so it was not so easy to pinpoint individual targets. Duc Thuy and his comrades were also on the ground. Anh Thuy crawled over beside Duc Thuy in the mud. "We must get closer," he said. A Marine drew his arm back, then brought it forward, hurling a grenade. It fell short, far to Thuy's left, then went off.

Thuy jumped up and ran forward, disappearing behind a hooch. He went up several hooches and came around toward the front again. In one hand he carried a long handled Chinese Communist hand grenade. When he was within range, he threw it toward the prone Marines. A moment after it exploded, Anh Thuy and the others got up and bore down on the Marines. The

Marines had not risen further than their knees before the guerrillas reached them. Several were shot: the others were bayoneted with the bladeless, long pointed knives characteristic of Chinese SKS carbine rifles.

Thuy and his comrades now scattered among the office hooches. From there they were able to fire at random on the perimeter from the inside. This caused considerable confusion among the Marines and broke their line of defense. For they were getting it from both sides, and the guerrillas inside the perimeter, though relatively few in number, were scattered in such a manner as to become difficult to subdue. They also had a clear line of fire on the defending Marines. In effect, their efforts at the moment were more deadly than those of the several hundred pressing upward toward the wire.

Someone shouted orders in English and the Marines began to pull back, heading down the trench and hooch line in the direction opposite that from which Thuy and his comrades had come. Alongside and to the rear of the Viet Cong several groups of Marines burst out of the French fort, firing their weapons on automatic as they came. They did not want to be trapped inside the concrete bunker, lest the guerrillas should choose to blow it up. Shooting steadily, they went right through the row of hooches past the Viet Cong, some of them dropping as they went. The majority of them were able to join up with the others beyond the hooches toward the motor pool. Duc Thuy reflected, as he took carefully aimed shots at the fleeting figures in the dark, that it was unfortunate none of the mortars had made a direct hit on the ammunition dump. The airborne flares had long since descended or burnt themselves out. The dark, mud and rain all came together as a single cold substance.

There had been, in the final moments of the main line guerrilla assault, a great deal of commotion, as they breached the wire and fell upon the bunkers and trenches. But no one was in them. Regrouping, they fanned out toward the office hooches where they met their comrades. From them they learned that the Marines were regrouping towards the motor pool. The guns fell suddenly silent and the rain washed over them in utter blackness.

The North Vietnamese commander now took control. Knowing there was little time to lose, he formed the men for another line assault. He could not be sure of the Marine defense, but he knew it would be hasty, improvised without the advantage of high ground or fortifications. They would even have to watch their ammunition expenditures now, since the ammunition dump lay between them and the communist forces. As Thuy prepared to move forward, he felt a sense of rising pride. This was a great victory for the people's army. It was not necessary to win battles to defeat the enemy, but when it could be done, all the better!

The North Vietnamese commander gave them the order to move forward. No time must be lost. Every moment's delay was to the advantage of the Marines and whatever superior firepower they could put into use. It was only the complete unexpectedness, great efficiency and extreme celerity of the guerilla assault which had ensured so far the unavailability of air support for the Marines. The aircraft had to come from Da Nang seventeen miles away and might well be only temporarily engaged in other missions.

The comrades got up en masse, stooped slightly over their bayoneted weapons. No effort was made now to lay down a covering base of fire. Rapidness of execution was essential.

The guerrillas did not shoot. They moved forward at a quick slog through the mud. They began to almost run in a long frontal line. A pop flare went up from the Marine side. It lit them up in an open area perhaps not more than fifty yards from the Marines. Then a machine gun began to swing back and forth along the communist left flank. Thuy could see comrades falling as the flare went out and enveloped him in darkness again, but he kept on going. M-16s were popping from the Marine side; a few of his comrades were firing. Thuy could hear the whine of bullets. He heard them slap into flesh. Anh Thuy was running alongside him.

Then there was a terrific flash followed by a roar. What he heard now among the ranks of his comrades was not an isolated gasp or moan here and there, but screams. Several more flashes came, one right after another, followed by explosions. Then Thuy remembered the ontos. It was the battery of big recoilless rifles on the ontos, firing at them singly pointblank.

The forward thrust of the Viet Cong assault was broken. The center of their ranks was a searing hole of burning flesh and crying moans. Now a withering hail of bullets poured down on them. The men scattered, heading for the perimeter on Thuy's right. They retreated up to the point where the earlier assault had breached the wire, and they now poured back over that wire and down the hill.

When events take a decisive turn toward defeat and annihilation, it is best to save as many of the people's fighters for tomorrow's battles as is possible. Dead guerrillas do not fight and cannot help anyone resist aggression.

XI

The first light of dawn did not find Duc Thuy far away. The sky was a sheet of gray but the rain had stopped. He could hear the whack-whack-whack of helicopter blades and the rattle of machine gun fire pouring down from the helicopters. In fact, from his position in a reedy patch in the river not more than two hundred yards downstream from the Marine compound, he had been able to see the thin red lines of the tracer bullets streaking downward in the pre-dawn night sky. Even now he knew many comrades had been lost and more were being added to their numbers. Twice he had had to sink down among the reeds in the muddy water, which was turgid from the rains, and breathe through the hollow reed tube he was carrying. This was when Marine patrols passed on either bank. The Marines were everywhere, like ants, both flying and on the ground. The so-called R144th North Vietnamese Army regiment was in full flight and disarray. But every man knew how to take care of himself, and somehow many would get through. The survivors would come together at various agreed upon rendezvous points later.

The Marines would count this a victory, but they would not forget their losses. For the Americans had a negotiable commitment, always to be rehashed and worked out. This was not their home. Their families did not suffer as did the rural Vietnamese. The people's army was prepared to endure whatever was necessary for however many years that were required.

Duc Thuy spent the entire day in the reeds and bushes along the river. He could not move away from there until well after dark. But the setting sun brought increased safety for the Viet Cong. When Thuy pulled himself out of the water he thought of staying for a few days with Quoc Duong Li, the contact man in the village of Dai Loc. It would give him a chance to rest and apply a poultice to his wound. But the injury was not serious, merely a flesh wound that had become a little inflamed from contact with the dirty river water, and Thuy remembered what he had observed in the rush of retreat. As he and his comrades had poured back across the perimeter and down the hillside, they could clearly see the village on both sides of the river. Many of the thatch huts were on fire. Between the descending flares and incendiary tracer bullets on the one hand and the counter-mortar shell fire on the other, anything flammable was not likely to be left untouched. People could be seen running back and forth on the village streets between the red flames. Not much, in fact, was left intact, just a few thatch houses that had somehow miraculously escaped the flames and some of the more durable French colonial buildings. Everything else was being consumed. It was obvious that Duong Li had not escaped his share of troubles.

Nevertheless, though deciding not to trouble Duong Li or take the risk of remaining under the noses of the Americans at this time, Duc Thuy did repair along the village street on the bank of the river opposite the Marine compound. This was the street on which the mortar tubes had been erected. The village was a shambles, since almost all the thatch houses had burned and some of the French buildings were missing parts of their walls or tile roofs. People were now crowded into the remaining structures, sunk in exhausted sleep, lying side by side on the concrete floors. The rain came down in a light drizzle and entered through the breaks in the roofs and walls. But the villagers slept on. Thuy slipped cautiously up the street. Marine ambush patrols might well be anywhere tonight, for they knew many Viet Cong were still in the area. He passed a building that must have served some sort of governmental function for the district headquarters, for there was a large pile of corpses stacked against its outer wall. These were bodies of his comrades. He did not look to see if Gia Ky was among them.

Towards the end of the street Thuy heard a light moan. As he stopped to listen, a small brown dog approached, its hackles raised. It was growling and seemed prepared to bark. But upon sniffing him, it wandered off to inspect the debris of a burned hut. Almost all that was left of that hut were two bunker holes that had been positioned under beds. Also among the ashes of burnt wood and thatch were the green remains of parts of some bamboo poles. The voice Thuy heard was that of a young woman. It came from inside an undamaged building. At first it seemed as if she were sobbing alone among her sleeping neighbors. But then a much stronger, clearer wail rose up beside her voice. Another joined it. In the rain mist into which the perpetrators of these events had mostly fled and dissolved, the women keened.

By long degrees and much effort spent in hiding in rivers, fields, rice paddies and patches of jungle, Thuy made his way back to the dense green jungle covered hill country. Here he wandered about for days, weakened by the exhaustion of his rice supply and his fear of showing himself to obtain food from any villagers. He had not attempted to reach any of the rendezvous points he had been informed of but had headed straight for the hill country. For his wound, though slight in itself, was now infected, badly festering. He staggered with a limp and felt feverish, wondering if it was because of the sun, since a few days of clear weather had intervened. Day and night the hills boomed, resounding now and then perilously close with the rattle of small arms fire. Once he found himself so near to a firefight in the dense jungle, he could hear shouting in the sharp, unmusical tongue of the Americans. But he saw nothing. He lay still for hours until the noise stopped, then backtracked a way before continuing onward.

Thuy was going from underground bunker to underground bunker, finding the caverns empty. One had obviously been cleared out by Marines, as there were rotting corpses in it. Thuy did not even attempt to enter it, the stench was so great. It was strange, he thought, that there should be such a slight Viet Cong presence now in these hills. They had long served as a major staging area for operations in the adjacent lowlands. The Marines must have finally realized where so many of the guerrillas were coming from, he reflected.

But he was beginning almost not to care. Soon he would be unable to travel. He lay down often on the cool, moist, forest floor, the floor of the jungle he truly loved, though he had learned something of its treachery in recent months; and he dreamed strange things. His mind was full of pictures: Gia Ky still alive in some American or South Vietnamese Army prison camp; men questioning him; someone pulling out what turned out to be his—Thuy's—own tongue. He was thirsty now and slept in fits, traveling as much as he could, penetrating deep into the jungle along familiar trails. For two days he had not even come upon a fresh pool or stream of water.

Then the clouds opened again, misting the tops of the trees, gathering further down into droplets of rain on bushes, vines and leaves. He found a clear area near the crest of a hill, an area burned over probably by napalm, and lay down, his face to the sky. He did not care that the tiny, stinging droplets of falling mist soaked him through and had brought with them a temperature drop of almost twenty degrees. A large, hairy, brown, tarantulalike spider crawled over his chest, and he did not attempt to brush it away. What did it matter if it was poisonous? So was he now. It would probably die if it bit him. It crossed over him and crawled away into the thick vegetation that had sprung up in the clearing. Then Thuy dreamed of a little brownish black snake with yellow and white markings. It bit him on the arm while he was sleeping in a clean hammock. He laughed as he carelessly flung the deadly reptile away.

On the following afternoon, still moving ever more deeply into the hill country, knowing he could now expect to find no form of help unless he came across some comrades, he entered, painfully, a bunker hole and found several men in the cavern below. One of them called for a nurse, and a young girl came and began to dress his wound. He was there for a week and, though he did not know these particular Viet Cong, they never left him. They prepared him food and drink; a surgeon opened and drained the wound; and the young girl, slender like his sister, Chi Lan, applied poultice after poultice to his wounded left hip. He never got her name or knew the unit of the men who helped him. When he was well enough to travel, though still with a limp but with the infection subdued and the fever gone, he awoke one morning in one of the larger underground caverns where he had been treated and found himself alone. Several weeks supply of rice lay neatly tied in bundles beside a near wall, and a canteen filled with water and attached to an American cartridge belt was included with them.

~ 79 ~

XII

Thuy's home village was much the same as it was when he had last seen it. The pace of life was slowed somewhat by the muddy conditions and relative coldness of the weather, but the eternal routines of communal and agricultural life went on. Thuy arrived in midmorning, found his mother not in the hamlet and was advised to seek her down by the river. There he found her with several other women, pounding the black and white cotton fabrics of the simple, ubiquitous, peasant's pajamas with a large rock. She would pound the water out of a garment, laying it against a larger rock and hitting it with the stone in her hand hard enough to squeeze out the water and dirt but not enough to beat a hole into it. Then, after making a round of several different pieces of clothing, she would dunk them all again in the slow moving water of the river. She repeated this process several times as he stood and watched her in silence. One of the other women finally noticed him and said, "Your son has returned."

Thuy's mother turned toward him, a smile of joy and surprise in her eyes and on her red betel nut stained lips: "It is in the goodness and silent motions of things that you have been brought home to me this day. I have wondered about your safety and longed for your return."

"My heart is at peace now that I see you again, mother," Thuy answered. "Where are my father and sister, Lan? I did not see them about the village."

"Your father has passed away."

"Of the fever?"

"Yes."

"Was there long suffering, much weakness and fatigue? He seemed to be getting stronger. I thought the fever would pass, as it has so many times before."

"It did not pass, and there was enough suffering to kill him. Your sister cared for him gently and looked after her mother as well. She is a strong girl, though not given to much gaiety or carefree talk."

"Where is she, mother? I wish to see her. I have thought of her much. A young nurse much like Lan took care of me when I was wounded and sick."

His mother looked at him questioningly: "You will not find her in the village. She has gone off to become like your nurse." A tone of bitterness edged her voice, but the light remained in her eyes. "The American war has taken my children away from me," she said.

"As it has many people," Thuy added. His mother had gotten up onto her feet from the squatting position she was in, and he placed an arm gently around her. She seemed bone thin and as light as a feather, but then he reflected that she had seemed so when he returned the last time as well. His recollection of her strength and of her caring authority in his younger years always seemed to clash with the physical reality of her body when he returned from a period of absence.

"Do you know what company Lan is with, what district she is in?"

"No, I have not seen her since she left."

"How long?"

"I do not recall. It has been many days, but not long overall, I suppose. She went away with them soon after your father died."

"With whom?"

"A man like your Communist Party friend." She bent over to pick up the clothes. Thuy helped her gather them. Then they turned and walked together along the short, jungle trail that led to the hamlet. The clouds were lifted into a high silvery sheen, admitting a considerable but subdued light. Birds were raucous in the trees, and at their feet chickens scattered here and there pecking after the rich insect fare in the forest.

Thuy had learned from one of the other women on the river bank that it had been about a month since Lan had left. He remained in the village helping his mother and the neighbors. The old rhythms of village life gave a renewed vigor to the heart and mind. In their separate way they were the rhythms of the river, the forest, and the unseen movement in the covering clouds. As with life itself, the Xuong Ca river was, in body and movement, slow and deep. Its opaque, silt laden, brown waters, like the impenetrable haze above, expressed the unseeable mystery of events, the limitless transcendence of inexpressible meaning. A man could not understand it, and that was its strength. Acceptance of it was his as well.

Thuy's mother never asked him about the fighting he was in, and he did not bring it up. The questioning look in her eyes when he mentioned his sickness and wound remained unanswered. It would not do now to question the inexorable flow of events. One must continue to hope. Perhaps soon the Americans would be driven away.

Thuy remained in the village for a week. Another week passed. He felt the need to return to his unit, to find and rejoin it, but he could not choose a day to begin. One day in the middle of the third week, while repairing some of the thatch on one of the overhanging eaves of his home, he turned around and saw Anh Thuy. It was a moment of joy. The two men embraced.

"I had not known if you were alive," Thuy said.

"The Party is invincible," Anh Thuy replied with a grin.

"What about our losses? Were they great?"

"About a third of the company: eleven men."

"Gia Ky was one of them."

"Yes, I have come to tell his parents."

"I have already done so."

"Good. Then perhaps you are now ready to rejoin your comrades."

"I am ready."

On the following morning the two men left the village. Thuy knew the hard routines of life in the hamlet would not be easy for his mother living alone. This was in part the cause of his indecision about leaving. But Anh Thuy's arrival reminded him of the greater need of the people, of many mothers like his own. The company of Viet Cong was presently quartered at the regimental base camp in the area. Duc Thuy and Anh Thuy went there. Duc Thuy learned that his company would soon be returning to action. Anh Thuy also informed him of a decision: he, Duc Thuy, would not be going with it.

"We have decided to provide you with further training as a Party member," he said. His eyes were lit up with his own sense of pleasure in the fact. "You are quite young, but I have long considered it and have spoken about it to others. I have told them of your coolness and firm actions. We have need of such men."

There was no question in Anh Thuy's mind of Duc Thuy's acceptance. It was a promotion and an honor not to be taken lightly by a people's fighter. Duc Thuy did not hesitate to show both surprise and pleasure. "I am always prepared to serve the people," he said.

Several days later, setting out from the regimental base camp, he began the long journey through seemingly impenetrable jungle, for the rich tangle of verdure grew taller in the dark vaults and denser along the sun breaks of open paths and stream courses as he approached the highlands. He followed carefully chosen trails from jungle camp to jungle camp in his slow progress toward the border between Vietnam and Laos. In the latter country, at a Party headquarters located somewhere in the endless sea of unpeopled forest, beneath the occasional pounding of bombs but out of range of American or South Vietnamese Army troops, he would learn the greater subtleties needed for waging a war of total liberation.